William H. H. Rogers

Wanderings in Devon

William H. H. Rogers

Wanderings in Devon

ISBN/EAN: 9783337189884

Printed in Europe, USA, Canada, Australia, Japan

Cover: Foto ©Andreas Hilbeck / pixelio.de

More available books at **www.hansebooks.com**

WANDERINGS

IN

DEVON.

BY

W. H. HAMILTON ROGERS.

"The Past and Present here unite,
Beneath Time's flowing tide,
Like footsteps hidden by a brook,
But seen on either side."

LONGFELLOW.

SEATON:
PRINTED BY JOHN NEWBERY,
QUEEN STREET.
MDCCCLXIX.

CONTENTS.

—o—

WANDERINGS

IN

DEVON.

BEER AND ITS QUARRY.

"THE toun of Seton," saith Leland, who wrote about the middle of the sixteenth century, "is but a mene thing inhabited by fischarmen;" but we trow, if the zealous old antiquary could now once again open his eyes on the present attractions of this healthy, thriving watering-place, he would scarcely credit them; such has been the influence of improvement here of late years. The short branch railroad runs us down to the mouth of the Axe as its terminus, and lands us on "the myghty barre and rigge of pible stones," that so often stops the ingress to the little harbour, but otherwise forms the magnificent open beach for which Seaton is so famous. Before us rises the great red Haven Cliff, and the giant mass is reflected again in the glassy depths of the transparent Axe, that moves slowly along at its foot, pouring its limpid tribute, a few yards further on, at the "very smaul gut" of harbour—where now as of old "come in smaul fischar boats for socour"—into the great briny hand of Neptune.

A leisurely stroll across the expanse of beach, a passing glance up the main street of Seaton, and we halt at the other extreme end, where the stupendous and beautiful White Cliff rears itself before us with a sort of implied question as to our further progress this way. Singularly handsome in outline, a very *beau ideal* of the famed English white cliffs, it is composed of dazzling lime-stone, rifted into large block-like masses, some fallen portions of which lie in huge *debris* of confusion at its base, where, about and between, the waves hiss and churn themselves impotently into spray, whiter than the barrier that challenges their progress. Overhead, a bevy of sooty choughs are darting out and in from numerous "coignes of vantage" near the apex, chattering noisily,—while at some distance below, in mid-air, a solitary gull sweeps slowly on in grand and noiseless equipoise, his long wings glancing in the sunlight. A friendly winding stair reveals itself a short space off, and up this we carefully clamber, emerging at the top into the narrow lane leading from Seaton to Beer. Here, the road leads straight away up over the hill which forms the adjoining cliff, and is cut out of the solid rock, at a gradient literally as steep as the roof of a house. But another path invites our attention, threading along the extreme edge of the cliff, and we slowly and cautiously ascend, halting a few moments at the stile halfway up, to notice a quantity of scarlet poppies growing on a ledge in the face of the cliff, and looking like a band of glowing flame traversing the creamy limestone.

On the top. What a glorious prospect. To the left lies Seaton, and beyond it stretches away for many a mile the fertile valley of the Axe. Below, the brown curve of beach extends across to Axmouth with its white church tower and the grand hill of Hochsdun rising behind it. In front, the mighty expanse of sea, studded here and there with stray sails, and the long grey mass of Portland reaching out in the distant horizon; to the right,—

"Cape after cape in endless range,"

down almost to the Start.

Image of eternity,
  Thou boundless sea,
That profferest heaven thy clear pellucid brow,
  Where the golden sunbeams sleep,
And the soft winds moan their ceaseless lulling vow,
  Far o'er thy bosom deep!

What a feeling of isolation and un-importance

creeps over the soul as we stand solitary and thoughtful on the verge of a high precipice, while around and about, far as the eye can reach, is laid out in stupendous, passionless, immutability, the vast panorama of Nature. On the glorious prospect is written in indelible characters the eternal prerogative of its Maker—a thousand years are but as yesterday. But where will be the handful of frail breathing dust that now contemplates its beauty and stability, when such a yesterday shall have passed over its destiny? And yet:—

> "Dust thou art, to dust returnest,
> Was not spoken of the soul."

"Fine a'aternoon, Zur,"—said some one close behind me in full manly tones, "but zum-how or 'nother, thee plagey school of mack'el is gone out to zay again, wuss luck, and I've been watching 'um this dree hours, I'll warn't."

Lost in our reverie on the scene before us, we were quite unconscious of the contiguity of the living being who had thus quietly approached and was standing a foot-pace at our rear.

"True," we ejaculated with a half start, "but then my friend, you know that patience is the fisherman's chief virtue,—better luck to-morrow."

"That's it, Maister," said our companion, who was a fine specimen of a representative race—the English sailor — and none finer are to be found on the indented British shore than those of Beer, from their being accustomed to the deep sea fishery in their swift luggers — excellently trained, daring and intrepid, thorough seamen in every sense of the word, and as such eagerly sought after to man "Her Majesty's ships." A bronzed face, garnished round with iron-grey curly hair (over which shadowed the orthodox and comfortable sou-wester), red neckcloth, and long blue jersey, trousers dappled with tar, and rolled half way up the leg of a large pair of fishing boots. Such was the outward *personnel* of our companion, and discoursing briskly on marine matters and fishing prospects, with all things proper thereunto pertaining, we pleasantly wended our way down the circuitous path to Beer.

The first view of the romantic village that we catch in our descent from White Cliff, shews us a long string of small-roofed houses, ranged along the base of a narrow gorge or valley, bounded on either side with steep, hilly acclivities, and stretching down to the little cove or bay. But the track winds rapidly down the face of the cliff, and in a few moments we land on a square platform or promontory, which leads out from the main street of the village, yet at considerable height from the beach below. There we found three or four old salts in quiet conversation with a smart preventive man, who looked in this ancient and redoubtable head-quarters of smuggling, like a marine Othello, with "his occupation gone." Possibly the venerable mariners were regaling his ears with some of the stories of their youthful days, when the contraband traffic was in its full glory and activity,—when Jack Rattenbury, the Rob Roy of the West, and his daring companions in this hazardous traffic, performed exploits whose recital now almost savours of romance. It was thought nothing of in those times to take a trip across the Channel in one of their open boats, bargain with Monsieur for a cargo of tubs, and back again to Beer, hoping for the chance of a favourable "run,"—a piece of luck which was rarely denied them. Careless of danger, and relying on their own consummate knowledge of seamanship, few accidents befel these adventurous sailors, who seemed in their persons and habits a cross between a sea-god and a free-booter. This was the era for—

> "A wet sheet and a flowing sea,
> A wind that follows fast,
> And fills the white and rustling sail,
> And bends the gallant mast;—
> The white waves heaving high, my lads,
> The good ship tight and free,
> The world of waters is our home,
> And merry men are we!"

Directly behind this platform is a delicious patch of green sward, where, to stretch ourselves at length, and quietly enjoy the scene, is but the work of an instant. Before us the little bay is circled like an ampitheatre. To the right the cliffs run out for a considerable distance, forming the head-land known as Beer Head; inside which is accounted one of the few safe anchorages in this terrible bay of south-westerly gales and a lee-shore. On our left is the noble cliff from which we have just descended. Ere we arise, however, some beautiful flowers of a little vetch attract our notice, which are spread thickly over the green, and whose intensely rich golden-bossed blooms, look as if they had been shaken from the girdle of some fleeting fairy.

We soon find our way down to the beach below, stopping for a moment to admire the little cataract that pours down the rock, some forty or fifty feet from the village above, and vanishes forthwith in the shingle beneath. A number of noted Beer trawlers are hauled up just above high-water mark, with sails, stores, and nets all aboard and in trim for the next day's venture. From one of these, as we pass, the clear tones of a fisher-boy, singing a popular refrain, catch our ear. We draw off a yard or two to get a glimpse of the joyous roysterer, and there he lies on his back, stretched at length on a pile of nets, with his sou-wester hat drawn over his eyes, to keep the sun off, and his legs and feet mounting up and down in the air, beating time to his song, while just below, a pair of ruddy arms, with hands clasped, lean on the gunwale, and on them rest a sweet face, surmounted with an unkempt profusion of bright fair hair, 'neath which a pair of mild blue eyes keep an unconstrained watch on the passers below. Surely, we thought, here is the Laureate's happily conceived picture of a verity:—

> "O well for the fisherman's boy
> That he shouts with his sister at play,
> O well for the sailor lad
> That he sings in his boat in the bay."

and as we looked at the merry lad, and then at the smiling sea, the inward prayer flashed across our heart, that another scene, described by the same powerful pen, may never be consummated in his fate—

> "Boy, though thou art young and proud,
> I see the place where thou wilt lie;—
> The sands and yeasty surges mix,
> In caves about the dreary bay,
> And on thy ribs the limpet sticks,
> And in thy heart the scrawl shall play."

God forbid! said we, as we passed down to the tidal marge, where tiny wavelets are crisply curling along in unrestful glee. Here a true Beer incident was in store for us. A trawler had just made the shore, and a little knot of fishermen were busily unloading her finny treasure. Three or four were half-leg deep in the water by her side, landing the fish, one or two others on the beach sorting them over, and engaged in an animated wordy warfare with a couple of those amphibious-looking bipeds, known as "chouters," chaffering, gesticulating, and bargaining with great energy for the less valuable portion of the catch, the best being carefully placed aside to be forthwith packed and consigned elsewhere by railway. Quietly, but interestedly watching the proceedings of the marketers, was a tidy, well-grown young woman, evidently the wife of one of the fishermen, which latter surmise was well attested by the vivacity of a chubby little boy, some two summers old, whom she was carrying, and who, guiltless of hat or shoe, was plunging and crowing, and with extended arms, endeavouring by every possible means to arrest the attention of a stalwart figure in the boat. Another group a short distance beyond completed the picture—three patient asses, nose to nose, with great panniers on their backs, stood lazily munching a small bundle of provender, and waiting the issue of the little trading venture, their large ears busily flapping away the plague of flies that continually tormented them.

On the east side of the short beach, at the base of the limestone cliffs, there rushes out from a large fissure in the rock with considerable volume, one of the most beautifully clear springs of water it has ever been our fortune to witness. Making use of the first drinking cup probably ever invented by man, the hollow of our hand, we quaffed with delicious satisfaction a good draught of Nature's bright and generous supply,

"Pure from the mountain urn!"

The natural advantages of Beer have, we believe,

on several occasions suggested the feasibility of forming a harbour of refuge here; but nothing of late years seems to have been actually proceeded with, yet Leland speaks of such an attempt having been made before his time:—"At Brereword," he writes, "is an hamlet of fischar-men. There was begon a fair pere for socour of shippelettes at this Brereworde, but ther cam such a tempest a 3 yeres sins, as never in mynd of men had before bene scene in that shore, and tare the peare in peces." About the beginning of the present century, Telford the engineer, surveyed the country between Beer and Watchet for the purpose of forming a canal, but the project was abandoned, and a railroad now traverses the district instead.

The main street, through which we stroll, consists of a long line of true fisherman's cottages on either side, with here and there a house of larger size, and somewhat more pretentious character. Beside the pavement runs down a channel filled with the produce of another of those magnificent springs of water that take their rise in the rocks around; and after supplying the place with a glorious plenteousness for culinary purposes, and the surplus acting as an invaluable sanitary commissioner, pours itself finally out over the rock at the beach.

The "inhabiters" of Beer are a fine well-built race; the men exceedingly frank and manly, and the women remarkable to a proverb in this part of the country for comeliness of figure and smartness of attire. A constant association with Nature in her various moods, exhibited to them in the vicissitudes and ventures of the fisherman's life, doubtless lends much of that innate nobleness of form and freedom of manner that distinguish them so notably in appearance from the pent-up city artizan, however skilful, who has always been inured to the sickly torpor and hot-house monotony of a town life. The *morale* of the village, too, is very satisfactory, notwithstanding the number of little "publics" dotted up and down the street, and the supreme treasure of religious feeling and experience is largely shared in many a cottage in the place—that true and blest kinship which identifies them in all parts of their calling with their holy predecessors of Galilee. Happy England, methought, whilst thou art guarded by a cordon of such hearts as these Beer fishermen; they are of more importance to thee than a fleet of the most powerful iron-clads. Where—so defended—is the foe that would face thee?—

"They know not in their hate and pride
What virtues with thy children bide,
How true, how good thy graceful maids,
Make bright like flowers the valley shades,
What generous men
Spring like thine oaks from hill and glen.

What cordial welcomes greet the guest,
By thy lone rivers of the west;—
How faith is kept, and truth revered,
And man is loved, and God is feared,
In woodland homes,
And where the ocean border foams."

A look in at the strange little nondescript shaped church, which with our usual good fortune we find open; but there is nothing worth remembrance except a memorial to W. Starre, who died "of the plague" in 1646. This fearful scourge, no perfect diagnosis of which has survived the period of its dreadful visit, appears to have decimated our western valleys with terrible mortality. In the neighbouring parish of Colyton, out of a population which at that time could not have exceeded a thousand souls, there died in the two years 1645-6, of "the sicknesse," as the recording minister notifies in the margin of the grand old register, four hundred and fifty-eight persons.

There is, however, one noticeable example deserving record amid the congregation of small dwellings forming the village. This is the house of the Starres —an extinct, but once important family resident here, and joint lords of the manor with the Walronds. Their dwelling composed of stone, taken from the neighbouring rock, displays the picturesque peculiarities of the Tudor era, the front door having an arch of good proportions. Directing our eyes upward to the chimnies, we discern on one, the initials of the founder, "J. S." and on the other, his device or rebus, a star radiated of many points.

There *was* also (alas it has recently shared the fate of almost all our antient buildings), to be seen on an eminence near John Starre's old residence, a mediæval cruciform barn of large proportions. The walls were very massive, with occasional long narrow crenelated openings to admit light, and which also seemed to infer the building may have been intended for a temporary fortress, when "boes and arroes" decided the chances of war. In the front porch was a very high and wide pointed arch of sufficient size to admit the largest wain-loads of the husbandman, and it had left remaining a fine specimen of an open timber roof, almost entire. It was termed the "Court Barn" and probably in former times, was the general repository of the manorial harvest.

As we saunter up the street our eyes unconsciously wander into the open cottage doorways, and just inside, sits many a fisherman's daughter, with her lace pillow on her lap, busily and dexterously weaving the delicate and fragile fabric, so world-famed when linked with the singular misnomer of "Honiton" lace. The well recognised rustle and "click" of the "sticks" catch the sense, as we pass on, and it may be that the tasteful "sprig" which the bright eyes and nimble fingers of the maiden are slowly elaborating, is destined to deck the robes of Royalty itself—no uncommon occurrence—as the lace made at Beer, is of the very finest quality, and held in great esteem by Her good Majesty of these realms, who used continually to employ it in the attractions of her attire on festal occasions, previous to these later and sadder days of her widowhood, and it still constantly graces the persons of her Royal daughters. This "glorious raiment of needlework" is now as of old, the heritage of princesses—

"The Daughter of the King
Is glorious to behold;
Within her closet she doth sit
All deckt with beaten gold;—

In robes well wrought with needle
And many a pleasant thing;
With virgins fair on her to wait,
She cometh to the King!"

The way to the Quarry leads on from the main street of the village, and huge boulders of rock jut out from the sides of the path, covered with moss and ferns, and hoary and worn with the attrition of ages. We pass the pretty row of comfortable alms-houses and school erected (as a memorial on them informs us) by Judith Maria Baroness Rolle, last representative of the ancient family of Walrond, of Bovey, the olden lords of Beer—a lady whose memory is embalmed in the grateful traditions of the place by this and other acts of beneficence. A group of the foundation boys are congregated at the school-room door, and their quaint dress attracts attention—a suit of true navy blue serge, with round cap, and on the breast of the jacket is embroidered a red pater-noster cross. A short distance further brings us to two or three quarriers' cottages, and on the left, close by, a large cavernous-looking arch in the rock tells us we have arrived at the entrance of the celebrated Beer Quarry.

Provided with a pilot in the person of one of the quarry-men, and armed with lantern and candle, we enter its gloomy looking precincts, and a strange sight await us. We are in a veritable mine, extending a considerable distance underground. Galleries or passages, hollowed out of the solid rock, lead in various directions, some quite clear and others partially blocked up with the *debris* and refuse of adjoining excavations, and huge pillars support the roof. Few fossils are found, but occasionally some beautiful crystalline formations occur between the interstices of the beds. The quarry we are in now is the new one, as it is called, but must have taken ages to excavate. The old one is to the right, and is said to occupy a large extent.

What a sensation of awe and lonesomeness creeps over the mind, in finding itself thus so far underground, in the very bowels of the rock as it were—the damp cold feeling of the air, the oppressive silence, and intense Cimmerian darkness, all the more apparent from the imperfect red blink of the candle. Yet here, day after day the patient quarryman passes the long bright *outside* day, the best part of his existence, hewing and delving out the ponderous blocks, so that to him the quarry becomes a kind of second subterranean home. No stranger, we should presume, ventures into the labyrinthine maze of galleries without a guide—as no earthly aid could find the lost in such a place; but many of the Beer men are well acquainted with a large portion of the cave's ramifications, and legendary lore speaks of it as having been a great storehouse and fastness for smuggling operations in days gone by. Returning towards the mouth of the quarry, we are struck with the immense number of the *Pipistrelle* family, which in all their varieties make these dark galleries their head quarters during the day, and are seen hung up by their hooked heels to the sides of the cavern, sallying forth in swarms in the evening twilight.

Out once more into the daylight—ah! how beautiful is the sun—even oppressively so just now, until our eyes are schooled afresh to his grateful radiance.

The Quarry of Beer we take to be one of the celebrities of the county in its way, and is well worth a visit by the tourist who seeks to explore the remarkable places embraced in this interesting portion of Devon. Traces of the product of its dark recesses may be found in almost all the buildings of any size within a radius of many miles, and large quantities are annually exported. Geologically, we believe, the bed which furnishes such large supplies at Beer, rises again at Widworthy, seven miles off, where it has been worked, and the noted quarries at Bath are but a continuance of the same stratum.

The old quarry has been worked from eight hundred to a thousand years probably. Almost all the antient churches in the neighbourhood are partially constructed of its product. Where are the sturdy hands that through so many ages laboriously delved out its rocky contents, and the cunning fingers that subsequently deftly carved and fashioned the rough blocks into delicately shaped foliage, fretwork, and finial? The visitor who views with admiration the many-ribbed, bold, fan-like, groining of the roof of Exeter Cathedral—that noble conception of the munificent Quivil —those lengthening arcades poised so fairy-like aloft, yet withal seemingly imperishable in their beauty, —would scarcely imagine that it is composed of Beer stone. Such we believe is the case. And in our fancy's eye we can look back with admiration at the glorious perseverance that accomplished it, amid difficulties of such magnitude that nothing but the real influence of religious feeling, that most powerful of all incentives, could have surmounted them. Those were not the days of railroads, let us remember, with their wonderful facilities of celerity and easy transit—and Beer is distant some five and twenty miles from Exeter. Neither was it an age of roads of any sort, nor of wheeled carriages—the early dawn of the 14th century. No broad turnpike aided the heavily laden wain with its ponderous load,—nor was its humble coadjutor the parish highway threading its tortuous, well-rutted windings over hill and valley available, but only the narrow, obscure, and miry track-way or halter-path—and therefore the probability is, that the masses of stone were all carried to Exeter on packhorses, and we can easily picture the heavily-laden convoy slowly defiling through the green combes, accompanied by their drover churls, patiently plodding on till they reached the stupendous fane — still the chief ornament of our county — then slowly rising from the ground like a coral rock from the briny depths of the ocean.

> " From hence came buttress, shaft and stair
> From crypt and vaulting rising fair;
> And all that slender steeple too,
> That like a fountain in the blue
> Rises exulting; here the branch
> Of the great windows, dyed with blood
> Of martyrs that no time can stanch;
> The altar and the by-gone rood;
> The mullions, drip-stones, and the shrine;
> The pavement, long since trod away;
> And saints that in their long array
> Wait patient for the judgment day;
> And angels that still gazing smile
> Upon the abbot in the aisle,
> Who on the flat tomb lies in prayer."

Our return is by another route, and we pass Bovey, the ancestral seat of the Walronds, a cadet branch of the main house at Bradfield, whose last heiress was the Judith Maria of charitable memory, Baroness Rolle, and founder of the almshouses.

Relative to this antient and reputable family, the visitor will find in their chapel in the parish church at Seaton, the interesting memorial of an olden member thereof, with the effigies of the deceased clad in the half armour and trunk hose of the time of the Commonwealth, kneeling in prayer before a *prie dieu*—below is this quaint inscription, "composed" and "set vp" by his widow, who was a daughter of Sir William Pole, Knight, of Colcombe, the county historian, and who thus seems to have inherited in some measure, a taste for her father's literary proclivities—

"AN EPITAPH ON THE DEATH OF EDMOND WALROND OF BOWE, WHO WAS BVRIED SEP. 10, ANNO DOMINI, 1640, ÆTAT SVÆ 48; COMPOSED AND SET VP BY ANNE WALROND, HIS WIFE:

HERE LIETH THE BODY OF MY HVSBAND DEARE,
WHOM NEXT TO GOD I DID BOTH LOVE AND FEARE,
OUR LOVES WERE SINGLE WE NEVER HAD BVT ONE,
AND SO I'LL BEE ALTHOUGH THAT THOU ART GONE,
AND YOU THAT SHALL THIS SAD INSCRIPTI: VIEW,
REMEMBER ALWAIES THAT DEATHS YOVR DVE."

Bovey House is a small, plain mansion, of Jacobean origin apparently, and a strange gloom of desolation seems to invest it. Polwhele gives a graphic picture of its last residents, on his visit there about a century ago:—"On visiting Bovey," (says he) "a few years since, I was pleased with the venerable appearance of the house and every object around it. It was then the residence of Mrs. Walrond. There was something unusually striking in the antique mansion, the old rookery behind it, the mossy pavement of the court, the raven in the porch, grey with years, and even the domestics hoary in service—they were all grown old together."

As we came out at the end of the short lane we

turned to take a last look at the old deserted manse, and the few scattered trees forming the remains of the ancient avenue. The sculptured forms of the rampant leopards still support the escutcheon of Walrond on the pillars of the gateway; but where is the living representative of the name? And where is the name of him who wedded the last green branch of this ancient stock, whose wealth and influence in his day and generation had from their vastness become an adage in the county? Gone too, and a stranger comparatively represents them both.

Often thus, thought we, does the Supreme Disposer of events arrange it. The peer with broad acres boundless, and wealth untold, sighs in his state that no child of his love may place him in holy earth, or fill his honoured station—and shudders as he dreams of an extinct name and his time-hallowed heritage apportioned to an alien—while the cotter whose only fortune is his brawny arms, and his inheritance the sweat of his brow, sighs too, as he deposits his shining tools at the cottage door, and casts an anxious glance at the merry, careless phalanx bearing his name congregated on the path and step, and who straightway swarm round his knee in the little ingle corner, while the great brown loaf is frugally apportioned among them by his thrifty partner.

The red rim of the rising moon is just up-wheeling behind the "brown shoulder" of the distant hill, and a single star is tremulously struggling for existence in the long line of saffron sky. A great white owl has just floated stealthily round the corner, noiseless as a cloud, and, scared by our unlooked for presence, darted over the hedge with the celerity of magic. The grass-hopper is busily carolling at our feet :—

> " Singing himself to sleep
> Beneath some pleasant weed ; "

and all flowers and forms are fast merging into one soft neutral hue.

> " Homeward the soul's strong wings are bent ! "

Good night !

THE NEST

OF

THE MOHUNS AND CAREWS.

A RIDE in the early train on the South-Western Railway, and a fine May morning. Fine we say—that is, bright and sunny to be sure, but with a chastened freshness in the air, and a bluish keen tint in the sky just over the distant hill-line, that tells us the rime-powed ambassador of Winter, John Frost, Esquire, of that Ilk, has not received his final passport from the warm hand of Summer as yet. Never mind, it is wise to make the best of all things, and though the morning air be a little unseasonable, it braces the muscles and exhilarates the feelings, especially to one bound on a tramping excursion. In a large roomy "third-class" of course, for your pedestrian antiquary has a careful eye to expense, and moreover rather likes the bustle and social fussy amenities of the people's Parliamentary coach, to the straightened state of a first-class (even if he could afford it), or the too often would-be gentility of the second-rated vehicle.

Carefully stowing away the striped "market return" and settling in a corner, we take stock of our companions—cheerful farmers, knowing cattle-dealers, and grey-clad, wise-browed millers, form the majority of the male portion, and their talk is alternately of oxen, of corn, of butter, of the hay prospect, with wise nods and knowing glances, enlivened now and then with a robust laugh.

Two or three of the softer sex are interspersed—farmers' wives or daughters, evidently, with sober business faces, and fine well-flowered bonnets. On their knees capacious baskets, in whose vast depths the freshest butter and newest eggs are carefully freighted, while from one of the wickered receptacles the violent flutter of wings and scratching of feet, betray the fear of the frightened prisoners within, fat pullet or capon as the case may be; yet the fierce struggles for liberty in no wise disturb the story of the sturdy dame who holds them—she is deep in butter-lore; its probable price, and how much she shall make this coming season.

One, a younger damsel, sits silent and alone in the carriage corner, and from behind the convenient cob-webby mazes of a thick veil, is coyly ogling a rather good-looking youth nearly opposite, whose semi-military air, moustache, and spruce garb, joined to the good-terms-with-himself he is evidently on, completely deaden the influence of the furtive glances that dart from the bright-eyed battery opposite.

Thus conning the apparent characters of our fellow passengers, we pass two or three little trim stations, each of which contributes its quota to the living load, when suddenly we emerge from a deep cutting, and the broad fertile vale of Honiton stretches away before us.

Facing the eye, the dense beetling woods of Tracey spread down the slope. To the right the grand pyramidal hill of Dumpdon sits like a monarch in the valley, his mighty brow crowned with trees, while the green fields that mantle his sides seem fastened together by the white building, which looks like a clasp on his capacious breast. Below, the ancient borough lengthens along, a line of slate roofs and chimneys, over which a haze of ghost-like smoke is passing. A glance out of the opposite window shows us the old church of St. Michael, whose massive tower seems to look with disdain on the slender Norman apology that shoots up amid the houses below.

How we hug ourselves often on these imitations and restorations, save the mark! destructions too often, we should have said. Compare the attenuated nineteenth century example at Honiton with the towers of Warlowast at Exeter. How *real* was their work: the reflex of their thoughts of Him for Whom they built, because

> "They dreamt not of a perishable home
> Who *thus* could build."

"Ticket, sir," exclaimed a voice at our side as we were unconsciously marching out of the station door with the crowd, forgetful of delivering up the half of our necessary passport. "Right," said we, recalling ourselves back to the present, for our thoughts had been busily traversing the past in relationship to the places we anticipated visiting, joined with a running commentary of fancy on the probable appearance of the *terra incognita* we were about to explore.

Outside the official precincts, the old tower of St. Michael stood on the hill before us, like a finger of old Time beckoning us to visit. Although not set down in the programme of our day's peregrinations, we could not resist the appeal; and, in less time than it takes to describe it, we were vigorously wending our way up the church hill, past the wicket-gate of the yard, and up to the great door, which we fancied was the merest trifle ajar, and to our intense delight moved open with a slow creak as we gave it a stealthy shove.

We have noticed that we are often lucky, as we term it, in our visits to old churches—that is, some one is generally within the building, or near at hand. Either the village-clerk's wife, busily dusting the seats, creeps out like a ghost from some out-of-the-way corner, and after requiring with a curtsey (sometimes), your business, makes you welcome, and follows your footsteps with a copious running fire of wordy information on church and parish affairs; a small silver gratuity, and curtsey number two (sometimes), terminating the interview. Or else a dull and measured click salutes the ear from some distant part of the yard, sounding with strange evidence of lusty vitality amid the silent realms of the dead. Instinctively our eyes have followed the direction of the sound, and amid the surging hillocks, close by a heap of new raised earth, we see a pair of sturdy arms and a frost-fringed head, surmounted by the poor crooked mattock, arise out of and descending into the ground at regular intervals, and an involuntary sigh seems to escape us as we watch the preparation for the last resting of some wearied soul, who has laid down for ever by the dusty roadside of this troublous life. The man starts as we walk over quietly and accost him with the usual query, if he has the key of the church with him. Eyeing us with a complacently inquisitive glance, he answers, in the affirmative—"Ees, sure, sur; you'll find en there, jist besides my tother tools;" where sure enough it appears, as large as an old-fashioned dragoon's pistol. Strange suggestive company, we think—the great church key and the grave diggers tools; and we often reflect as we open the ponderous door, and hear the great hinges grate, how far distant is the time when they will turn on us, lastly and for ever!

We enter, and sit down in the cool calm to recover ourselves a minute; but our eyes are all astare at the sight of the gorgeous screen that stretches across the chancel. Ah! here again, is no modern sham, but real sturdy oak, carved into patterns of bewildering intricacy and richness—foliage, fruit, and flowers, groinwork, cusps and bosses: the cunning workman had no contract here; no "trades-union" threat to cramp his fingers or damp his ardour. He *saw* in his mental eye the pattern his hands gave an enduring and tangible evidence of; he *felt* the mysterious influence of the Great Master for Whose honour he laboured. Aye, these old workmen — the spirit of the Cross stamped alike the dignity of their labour in the Sanctuary as truly as its hallowed symbol was impressed upon their silver wage. Railroads, steam-engines and telegraphs, seem to make us forget such things now-a-day, instead of helping us to expand and enrich them, as their improved means should.

Over this elaborate band of carving, in place of the "Holye Roode Tree," with the semblance of Him Who was crucified for all, once displayed thereon—there now stands the gilded puffy diapasons of a modern organ—a nineteenth century embellishment of course.

Through the skreen-door—what is the legend on the chancel pillars?—

"Pray for ye souls of John Tackell
and Jone his wiffe."

Good old Jan and Joan Tackel!—"Blessed are the dead that die in the Lord,"—we answer to your appeal,—"for your works shall follow you."

The almost unconscious benediction had scarcely parted from our lips when an old gravestone in the north aisle caught our eye, whose nearly obliterated ledger line after some careful search, revealed the last resting place of the godly old Joan, then a widow—

"Hic jacet Johana Tackell vidua, que obiit xvi
die Julii Anno Domini MCCCCCxxx,
cujus aie propicietur Deus, Amen."

Taken altogether, however, there is much in the old church for the eye to dwell on with pleasure. It has not been tampered with as yet, and its old features thoroughly effaced by recent renovations.

We have often a great horror of these modern restorations, where zeal, set on fire with a little money, energetically destroys everything within its reach, and some venerable old pile perchance comes out as from a band-box; spick and span new, from the topmost pinnacle of the tower to the freshly added nose and moustache of the grim knight, who sleeps "stony sound" in the chancel, and whose mutilated limbs have been patched up to keep pace with the garish display of illumination blazing around. It won't do, believe us—your modern stone-mason's chisel destroys all charm of the past like the wand of a magician. A church should be a sort of kalendar of the past, where each succeeding century should be represented from its foundation, quite as much as a rallying point for the present. To break one link destroys the whole chain.

In order therefore, to preserve and perpetuate

this sequence of regard, with a reverend and cautious spirit the elaborate Elizabethan and Jacobean monuments, with their be-ruffed figures, beard-a-peak or mob-cap, array of heraldry and ornate epitaphs, should be scrupulously cared for :—the "*orate pro anima*" of the old Catholic vicar of the fifteenth century in the chancel floor, and the equally interesting one to the '*reverend and pious*' Puritan minister of the Commonwealth, whose heretical dust is covered by the adjoining stone—all have alike their interest, and claim to our common respect.

Aged 105! Who can this be? Let the quaint inscription on his tomb describe him—

"HERE LIETH THE BODY OF THOMAS MARWOOD,
GENT.; WHO PRACTISED PHYSICK AND CHIRURGERY
ABOVE 75 YEARS, AND BEING ZEALOUS OF GOOD
WORKS, GAVE CERTAIN HOUSES, AND BEQUEATHED
BY HIS WILL TO THE POOR OF HONITON,
10 POUNDS, AND BEING AGED ABOVE 105 YEARS,
DEPARTED IN THE CATHOLIC FAITH,
SEPTEMBER YE 18TH, ANNO DOMINI, 1617."

He was physician to Queen Elizabeth, and lived in a grand old house in Honiton, where he entertained the unfortunate Charles the First, while on one of his western journeys. The loyal and charitable old doctor seems to have well preserved his own life, whatever may have been his fortune with other people's.

A word by the way about the descendants of this

venerable court chirurgeon, who were lords of the adjoining parish of Widworthy; where two interesting old manses are found, Barton and Cookeshayes, their antient homes. In the parish church are several splendid memorials to these succeeding Marwoods—"*eminent for piety, honesty, and good œconomy.*" The last of the race died about fifty years since; the owner of such vast landed possessions that a saying was current with the country people to the effect that he had an estate for every day in the year—but sad and wondrous sequel—bereft of reason for many years before his death, he died the childless and unwitting possessor of almost boundless wealth.

A number of other memorials cluster about the walls, the short title pages to past histories, but of no special import.

We make our exit by the chancel door; but stay, what have we here? A brass plate, covered with extraordinary orthography, tells us—

"HERE LYETH YE BODY OF JAMES RODGE, OF HONINTON, IN YE COVNTY OF DEVONSHIRE, (BONE-LACE SILLER. HATH GIVEN VNTO THE POORE OF HONINTON PISHE THE BENYFITT OF £100 FOR EVER,) WHO DECEASED YE 27 OF JVLY, AO. DI. 1617, ÆTATE, SVÆ, 50. REMEMBER THE POORE."

He was probably one of the early introducers of the manufacture of this elegant material from Holland, which now gives such busy employ to the nimble-fingered maidens of the district. Very little lace, however, is now made at Honiton; its fabrication has migrated towards the sea-coast, where the fishermen's wives and daughters, living in the villages that skirt the shore between Axmouth and Exmouth, produce it in abundance.

We saunter down the yard, catching a glance at the names on the head-stones as we pass. Ah! what name is that? Edwin Flood, the most gifted scion of a gifted family, a genuine musician; among whose numerous beautiful productions not one bar of meaningless or careless music can be found. Only 24—just so—

"Whom the God's love die young."

The minor wail of the new church chime is tinkling in the valley below;· but another echo is ringing its sweet change on our inward ear at the sight of that name—the melody of the *Sabbath Bells*. Alas for earthly sabbaths, and those who sing of their hallowed associations, would they could have soothed

"The dull cold ear of Death:—

at least for a time, and this rare evanescence of genius been spared for many a year to delight and charm us! Yet who would keep those fairy fingers here, that now make eloquent the seraph's golden harp, in the endless Sabbath of the Blessed.

Once more the thought of the old church door and its hinges recurs, and recalls the words of the American poet, as we hurry away from the sacred enclosure:—

"Again the hinges turn, and a youth, departing, throws
A look of longing backward, and sorrowfully goes;
A blooming maid, unbinding the roses from her hair,
Moves mournfully away from amidst the young and fair.

Oh! glory of our race that so suddenly decays!
Oh! crimson flush of morning that darkens as we gaze!
Oh! breath of summer blossoms that on the restless air
Scatters a moment's sweetness and flies we know not where!

I grieve for life's bright promise, just shown and then withdrawn.
But still the sun shines round me, the evening bird sings on,
And I again am soothed; and beside the ancient gate,
In this soft evening sunlight, I calmly stand and wait."

Down over the hill at a canter, through New-street to the broad main thoroughfare of the town. All is a-stir; here a blue-smocked butcher is toiling along beneath the heavy burthen of a well-fed porker; there a cheap Jack is getting ready his splendid bargains; market gardeners display their vegetable stores; fishmongers, hollow-turners, basket-makers, and agricultural craftsmen of all descriptions are getting ready their stock of wares; for Honiton is *par excellence* a genuine specimen of a market town, for all "stand in the market," situate in High-street, to dispose of their commodities.

On the pavement a crowd of busy folks are hurrying along; in the street a herd of red-coated Devons are slowly edging on their way, to the reiterated shout of the drover, the long white horns of the bullocks glancing up and down in the sunshine. Behind them a patient convoy of heavy fleeced "grand Devon" sheep are labouring along, to the incessant clatter of an aged sheep-dog, which barks like a machine behind the portly presence of an old ewe in the rear, who, evidently from long acquaintanceship, is supremely contemptuous of his presence and prowess. Following these, at a short interval, comes a troop of divers-coloured swine, with erect ears, quick eyes, and snouts pointed to the ground, ever ready for contraries and mischief; anon halting and grunting, till the sharp snap of a powerful whip sends them on at a gallop.

Then, amid the wirling eddies of dust, ere we reach the turnpike on the Upottery-road, smart traps rattle along, knots of well-to-farmers amble leisurely by, with here and there the inevitable useful ass and low-wheeled cart, pattering steadily on, and drawing his cottage mistress to market, who sits in state upon a great maund of cabbages, that fill up the body of the little vehicle, while a bundle of neatly made besoms are lashed to the tailboard.

At last we gain the turnpike, thankful to leave the bustle and dust of the crowded street behind. The sun has now broken out in full blaze, and we saunter steadily on, vaguely surmising the direction we have to take, for our present stock of information ceases at a half mile *plus* the toll-bar.

While we are thus cogitating, an eddy of dust at a turn of the road anticipates the approach of something living, which soon resolves itself into the semblance of a stalwart farmer's lad, leading a heifer and calf to the market. The careful mother walks restlessly around, with soft loving low, her large eye anxiously glancing beneath her handsome creamy horns, as we stop the rustic leading her progeny, for further directions as to our future path :—

"Which is the nearest way to Mohuns Ottery, my lad?"

"Moons Awtrey you do mean, sir."

"Yes."

"Doo'e know where Munkkun Pown is, sir?"

"Yes."

"Well, when you comes there, turn down to the left, and vollee straight up auver the hill till you comes to a dree cross way, turn to the right, and that 'll lead right auver to Moons Awtrey."

"Thank you, my lad; good morning." A few hundred yards of steady pace brought us to the unmistakeable little walled enclosure, with wooden entrance hatch referred to by our trusty informant, and we struck at once down the narrow lane leading off to the left.

Right pleasant is it to leave the hot broad dusty turnpike road and find ourselves in the shadows and quietness of a true Devonshire lane, as this turn in our track proved itself. Over head the "Corinthian" elm spread her leafy skirts far and wide, or feathery foliaged ash, or strong-limbed oak, giving a welcome shade. Below in the hedge-sides, the wild flowers grew by myriads. Here a cluster of carmine-starred wake-robins started up, there a sweet honey-suckle trailed along, or fierce-armed dog-rose displayed his pale-pink blooms. Interspersed, were luscious butter-cups and pale silver-starred strawberry blossoms, while every now and then at intervals, the glorious fox-glove —that lover of "the west countrie," as old Leland hath it, shot up his spire of bells.

At the base of the hedge a bright rill sparkled along, fringed here and there with tufts of what in our ignorance of botanical nomenclature, we have ever known as *water* forget-me-nots, whose tiny quaterfoils of matchless turquoise hue, make it the gem of English wild flowers. Hovering over these, with dainty restlessness, was a troop of the smaller dragon flies, their gorgeous blue wings flashing like burnished armour in the sunlight. Great humble-bees bustled about on their busy errand; the birds were singing blythely, and crowds of gnats at intervals threaded their mazy dance under the shadow of some drooping branch.

At the foot of the descent lay a stone bridge, spanning one of those rivulets which are almost constantly found flashing rapidly along the bottom of the narrow green Devonshire combes. Erected apparently about a century since, with a tall arch which rendered the roadway over as steep as the roof of a house; its builders little dreamt of the unborn time of iron-girders and their level approaches.

A rest for a few minutes on the parapet, and a look down the valley, could not be resisted. Below, the stream bounded through the narrow archway with a sparkling run, or "stickle" as it is locally defined, which a few yards further on became spent, and amplified itself into a tolerably sized pool, skirted with tall reeds, over which drooped the darkling alder. Here the still surface was from time to time broken by those well-known circles which betokened the wakeful presence of the dappled trout, stealthily catering for his dinner from the quivering rout of flies that swarmed above him :—

> The speckled brigand of the stream,
> Moulded with beauty's line,
> Rich o'er whose breast of golden gleam
> The rays of Iris shine.

Spirit of glorious old Isaac! come forth and furnish us with our accustomed slender wat'ry store of pliant rod and yellow dun, that we may trap the quick-eyed rascal in his craftiness; for the blood of Zebedee hath possessed us utterly! Alas, for impossible wishes and impulsive intentions, they will not be gratified to-day.

An old-fashioned farmhouse, surmounted by a Tudor chimney, and a lane that stretches away up a steep hill, are before us. We mount leisurely, noting the beautiful ferns that clothe the hedge banks. Now glancing at the tiny serrated fronds of the maidenhair nestling at the foot of a huge stump, or the large, long, leathery leaves of the hart's tongue drooping from its summit, or stopping an instant to admire a grand tuft of the common fern, with its beautiful fringes, until at last we reach the "three-cross-way," described to us by our informant driving the cow.

Following on the lane to the right as directed, for a short distance, some grand old trees made their appearance at a sweep in the road, the advanced post as it were, of the manorial precincts. These trees from their large size, dwarfed the surrounding representatives of their kind in the neighbouring hedges, and were evidently of great age; while their ample foliage almost completely hid a small farmhouse from sight.

Not far from this, still pursuing our way, a large gate stretching across the lane, and the remains apparently of an avenue, tokened the near approach of Mohuns-Ottery—which a slight turn at a few paces further distance revealed at once.

Mohun! what a "strange, eventful" history is attached to that name. A cradlehood of glory—an exit of shame. The grand old Norman sire of the race lived in his castle of Dunster, and from thence his knightly lineage descended by divers strains in

Cornwall, Devon, and Somerset. The Devonshire Mohuns were famous for their pious beneficence—the abbey of Newenham being founded by them; soon after which it should seem the old coat armour of the family—*a sleeved arm, the hand holding a fleur-de-lys*—was exchanged for the noble device adopted by the abbots of Newenham—*a great gold cross on a sable field.*

The family lingered on to the days of Charles I., when the then head of the house was ennobled by the title of Baron Mohun, of Okehampton; but a sad extinction awaited its last representative, Charles, the fifth Viscount; who, after being twice tried for murder, found a bloody death in a duel with the Duke of Hamilton, when both antagonists were killed. The name yet lingers among the Devonshire yeomanry, derived possibly from some stray branch from the main stirpe, changed to the homely but celestial patronymic of *Moon.*

From the Mohuns the estate passed to the Carews, another noted Devonian race—"a right noble family," to use the words of Prince, the lustre of whose antient fame as soldiers and civilians stands out in marvellous relief, and is still bright and undimmed as ever. A short account of these worthies will be excusable, and we trow acceptable

Sir John Carew, the first of the race, settled here, having married the heiress of Mohun. He was a famous soldier, and fought at Cressy, dying in 1363.

The tomb in the chancel of Luppit church probably marks the sepulchre of this knight; a portion of the cusped arch remains, but the canopy it forms is tenantless of its former effigy—not to be wondered at, we think, as we glance at the *lime and sand floor* of the chancel, and desolate churchyard.

After Sir John came Thomas, his son, a valiant knight also, who was with the dauntless Henry V. at Agincourt. Another Carew, Baron Nicholas, great at the court of Edward IV., is, with his wife, sepulchred in the regal precincts of Westminster Abbey. John Carew was a daring seaman, under Henry VIII., and while commanding *The Regent* "engaged a French carrick of great force; they entered her, which, when her gunner saw, he desperately sate fire to the powder, and blew them both up, together with Sir John and 700 men." Thomas Carew, an equally bold soldier, was the English knight who at the field of Flodden took up the gage of the valorous Scottish knight, Andrew Barton, before the battle began, and vanquished him—a presage of the fate of the encounter that followed.

Others were famous men in the stirring times of Queen Elizabeth. George, the most celebrated, served his Royal mistress well in Ireland, who wrote to him as her "Faithful George," telling him that his services "should neither be unremembered nor unrewarded; while, believe my help nor prayers shall never fail you;—your sovereign that best regards you—E. R."

James I. created him Baron Clopton and Earl of Totness; and to quote farther from the pages of the gossipping Prince, he was "a faithful subject, a valiant and prudent commander, a honest councillor, a gentile scholar, a lover of antiquities, and a great patron of learning." His dust, under a stately monument, finds a resting place beneath the same roof that enshrines the peerless Shakespeare. Gawen, a distinguished courtier; Peter, a great soldier; and George, a learned divine, added their quota of brilliancy to the galaxy of chivalry and learning that distinguished the remarkable reign of the virgin Queen.

But it is time to bid adieu to the past and think of the present, for here we are before the "Nest" of all these knightly worthies. The large array of evidently new slate roofs gives the worst anticipations of what we shall find on a nearer approach—that the old house has given place to a new one. Such indeed is the case.

While we were inwardly lamenting, however, all at once we were surprised to find ourselves before a fine old arched gateway, through which as we looked, at a short distance behind, was another such arch, while further again beyond appeared the deeply-moulded and hooded arch of the front door, inside which was again another curved doorway, forming a strikingly beautiful gradation of distances; and which, with a living figure or two, would have formed a glorious stereograph. Clusters of roses hung from the wall-sides, interspersed with myrtles and jasmines, while tufts of great Whitsun gilliflowers, and other old-fashioned sweet blooms, rose in profusion from the border that lined the passage.

A knock at the door soon brought out the worthy occupant, with an invitation to rest, and the Devonshire farmer's welcome of a glass of sweet sparkling cider.

"A new house, my friend," said we, looking about —"have you lived here long?"

"More than fifty years," replied he; and to our other query, "it *is* a new house; the old one, a fine old place, with large stone windows, was burnt down about twenty years since; when nothing was left but the front porch and the old arches of the gateway."

Refreshed with our rest, we sallied forth to scrutinise the few ancient remains left.

At the rear of the building we found one of those immense fire-places, yet left remaining in our antient baronial residences, (notable similar examples to which also exist at old Shute House and Colcombe), whose enormous ingle corners stretch from one side of the room to the other, and are literally big enough to roast an ox in, if required.

Over the front door are the initials "P. C." being those of the Elizabethan soldier before referred to, and in the spandrils of the front arch, amid a profusion of elegant scroll-work and foliage, with their proper supporters, on the one side are the arms of Carew, whose *three lions passant guardant,* seem to challenge the royal ensigns for distinction; and on the other side the early *maunch* of Mohun, *bearing the fleur-de-lys.*

Not far from the house is the site of what was probably once a fish-pond, or reservoir, of large dimensions and great depth. On one side are the remains of a strong flint masonried culvert for carrying off the superfluous water; the place is now all overgrown with trees and coppice wood.

Ere we returned, the loan of a chair and our sketch-book gave us a half-hour's pleasant occupation, to the intense curiosity of two plough-boys, who were keenly eyeing our proceedings, one mounted on the top-most bar of a gate at our rear, and the other from the crest of the gateway before us, whither he had clambered and sat himself down, peeping out from the dense mass of ivy, like Minerva's bird of wisdom.

THE CRADLE

OF

MARLBOROUGH.

A KEEN, cold morning, a veritable winter one—quiet and undisturbed—when the air holds a kind of constrained stillness, as if frost-bound. The hard turnpike road reverberates under the tread, as if it were composed of one continuous piece of granite, stratified with threadings of iron, indicated by the dark stripes of water congealed in the wheel-tracks. Twig, branch, and briar are white with the wondrously beautiful frost rime, and the grass, covered with the silvery crystallisation, crackles crisply beneath the foot. It is hard times with the smaller birds, who scarcely care to move out of one's way; and a great grey thrush, with plumage ruffled up and a very mendicantish look, has just brushed over the hedge, scarce a dozen feet in front of us—let us trust he may soon recover his minstrel suit and sweet voice, with the advent of bee and cuckoo.

Such was the general appearance of things on the short stretch of road lying between the little rural village of Whitford in Shute, and the handsome skew arch of the railway at Woodhayne. There our route diverged from the turnpike; and, crossing the Axe on a narrow wooden plank, the path lay over the meadows.

The Axe! bright, sparkling, many-curved Axe, queen of these eastern streams, how many delightsome associations conjure themselves into being within the busy brain at the sight of thy murmuring tide! Of olden time, when the royal Athelstan and his armed legions waded thy waters in surging conflict with the invader's host, crimsoning thy pure bosom with the carnage,—of the minster founded on thy bank in memory thereof, by the same regal mind, and whose grey tower, now peering down the valley through the clear morning air, preaches to us still the eternal purpose of the founder—and makes the thousand years that have passed since that tower was first upraised, appear even to our finite minds, but comparatively as yesterday.

A succeeding age witnessed two small companies of serge-clad, shoonless monks, halt upon thy marge, meeting there the belted nobles of the district, and with solemn ceremony, together laying the foundation stones—cross-graven—of two noble abbeys. Again, after a dozen fleeting generations had passed, didst thou see the successors of those holy men, with heavy, grief-bowed hearts, hand over these grand fanes, the refuges of piety and learning, and reared in honour of the Chief Corner Stone, to the mercenary and greedy favourites of a lawless, remorseless king. The mocking shadow of one still exists to attest its high-born origin—the other, long since razed to its foundations, is now the home only of the mole and the bat. The Royalist, the Roundhead, and eke the hapless partizan of Monmouth, have, in turn, alternately forded thy shallows, till now of late the iron-road hath spanned thy lisping marge, and the snorting monster, with his cohort of living freight, whirls with savage energy along thy babbling precincts. Yet, gentle river, shall thy sweet silvery sparkle out-run them all—

> "For men may come, and men may go,
> But you go on for ever."

And—ever sacred—for thine own blest natural delights, glad stream, how prized art thou—thy rich-tinted flags and rustling reeds, thy swallows and daisy-sprent banks, thy mirrored reaches, and thy bounding stickles—

> "With here and there a lusty trout,
> And here and there a grayling."

Pleasant and healthful is it (for mind and body alike) to pursue the "contemplative recreation" of the grand old Isaac on thy banks, drinking rich draughts of Nature's sweet communion, lost in delicious dreams and tranced reveries—(nervously disturbed, however, now and then at intervals by a vigorous twitch at your furthermost blue upright)—and during a live-long afternoon, follow quietly thy convolutions, revelling onward as it were reluctantly through the dappled meadows, till the retreating golden sunlight of evening blushes its last farewell.

Splash! splash! whirr! whirr! whirr!—Ah! there they go; a magnificent mallard towering up, and a couple of ducks after him. Look at his gorgeous green glossy neck, iridescent in the sunlight, and otherwise splendid plumage, contrasting with the ruddy breasts and sober colours of the ducks. Up, up, up,—and now away with vast speed down the valley to their ocean fastness, lessening even already to three dark specks in the cool ether.

"Drat it, Maister," said a voice in pure vernacular, from a fustain coat and shapeless wide-awake creeping out from a corner of a hedge, "I wish 'ee hadden a come on for half a minnit, I should a had a couple of 'em, I'll bet a ginnea."

"Never care, my man," said we, "they are happier where they are; and, you *may* have another chance this evening."

"Perhaps," we continued *sotto voce,* and inwardly hoped he might, as we eyed our sporting companion's "fowling piece"—an antique specimen that had evidently been carefully treasured as the heir loom of the cottage dynasty for generations, and had probably made the peaceful echoes of this valley reverberate every winter with due regularity for the past half century.

Thus, fair birds, this morning we have been the

unconscious agents of your safety—the bearers of your reprieve it may be from death, or your lustrous wings from ghastly maims—a gracious errand that ye wot little of, as ye bask securely 'neath the crest of the curling billows. To day at least—

"Vainly the fowler's eye
Might mark thy distant flight to do thee wrong,—
As darkly painted on the crimson sky
Thy figure floats along.

Thou'rt gone,—the abyss of heaven
Hath swallowed up thy form;—yet on my heart
Deeply hath sunk the lesson thou hast given,
And shall not soon depart.

He who from zone to zone,
Guides through the boundless sky thy certain flight,
In the long way that I must tread alone,
Will lead my steps aright."

But stay, here we are in a large park-like field, aptly enough named *Vernal* in the sweet spring-tide approaching; and there is Ashe House, beneath whose roof, so peacefully situate in these sylvan solitudes, one of the mightiest and most successful of English soldiers first saw the light.

The family of Drake of Ashe, from whom maternally, Marlborough was descended, is of considerable antiquity; and the first of that name located here, migrated from the parent stock at Spratshays, near Exmouth, about the beginning of the sixteenth century. This John Drake, among other offices, held that of steward of the conventual estates of the abbey of Newenham, under abbot Gyll, at the time of the dissolution of these religious institutions, and doubtless had his share of the plunder. A few descents from the aforesaid John, came Bernard, a distinguished seaman of a noted epoch, rich in fruit of these old Devonian sea-lions, and associated with Hawkins, Gilbert, Raleigh, and others.

Prince relates a characteristic story of this sturdy sailor :—" There fell out (says he) a contest between Sir Bernard and the immortal Sir Francis Drake, chiefly occasioned by Sir Francis—his assuming Sir Bernard's coat of arms; not being able to make out his descent from his (Sir Bernard's) family; a matter in those days, when the court of honour was in more honour, not so easily digested. The feud hereupon increased to that degree, that Sir Bernard a person of a high spirit, gave Sir Francis a box on the ear, and that within the verge of the court. For which offence he incurred her Majesty's displeasure, who bestowed upon Sir Francis a new coat of everlasting honour to himself and posterity for ever. And what is more, his crest is,—*a ship on a globe under ruff, held by a cable rope with a hand out of the clouds; in the rigging whereof, is hung up by the heels, a wivern gules,* Sir Bernard's arms; but in no great honour we may think to that knight, though so designed to Sir Francis. Unto all which Sir Bernard boldly replied :—' That though her Majesty could give him a nobler, yet she could not give an antienter coat than his.' "

Very boldly and very pluckily replied, too, think we, in those critical times of the headsman's block, and an imperious woman's resentment, so significantly implied by the disgraced wyvern. The irate Master Bernard soon found, or rather fought his way back into her Grace's favour, "who revolving in her Royal breast the many good services he had also done her," knighted him in 1585. But poor Sir Bernard! a sad end awaited him—a sequel illustrative of this age of chivalry and inhumanity. He was the unconscious author of his own death, and in a most singular manner.

Sir Bernard, in one of his buccaneering expeditions, took a "Portugal ship," and carrying his prize into Dartmouth, the poor native seamen were forthwith transferred to the horrors of confinement in the gaol of Exeter; to be there "closely and nastily kept," to use the phrase of the great Lord Bacon animadverting on what occurred after this very case. His captives landed, home hurried Sir Bernard, and soon after hied him down to Exeter to attend the assize where these pitiable prisoners were to be arraigned. Serjeant Flowerby sat in judgment, and when the poor sickly emaciated wretches were brought up for trial, there "suddenly arose such a noisome smell from the bar," that the judge—Sir J. Chichester, Sir A. Basset, and Sir B. Drake, sitting with him, eleven of the jury, and many other people in the court, sickened and died of the infection! Sir Bernard, however, had strength sufficient to rally; return to Ashe, and expire there a short time after.

What a ghastly picture of the habits and want of forethought and humanity of men at this time, who generally appear to our view, through the kaleidoscope of time, as instinct with nobleness, courage and generosity. But this is a peep behind the tinselled curtain, which awaited the benign hand of Howard fully to raise and finally expose such aggravated horrors to the withering glance of merciful indignation, a century afterwards—

> "Howe'er it be, it seems to me,
> 'Tis only noble to be good."

But *apropos* of Sir Bernard. Let not the visitor who comes this way, after he has looked at Ashe, forget to set aside an extra half hour to visit the little church of Musbury, where the Drakes are buried. There he will see three pairs of kneeling figures, life size—each a knight and his lady—in themselves, together, the most striking array of the kind to be found possibly in the county. The knights in complete suits of armour, richly inlaid, with massive gold chains and crimson scarves, cropped polls, ruffs, peaked beards, and the expression of their faces evidently giving strong warrant of their being likenesses. The central figures of this group represent the courageous, fever-stricken Sir Bernard, and his wife Gertrude Fortescue, of Filleigh, who is attired similarly to the other two ladies, in long black gown, with rich gold embroidered stomacher, ruff and mob-cap. The grandson of this Sir Bernard was Sir John of that name, "who had to wife" Elinor, the daughter of Lord Boteler, of Bramfield. He was the father of Mary Drake, the wife of Sir Winston Churchill, Knight—of Minthorne, Dorset—and mother of Marlborough, who was born here, on Midsummer-day, 1650.

Thus much for our hero's pedigree, here we are at the door of his birth-place. Only a portion of the old mansion is left, nearly about the exact half. The original fabric, in its completeness, was E shaped; of this, one wing and part of the centre remain. The building is lofty, with Tudor windows, and contains a large dining room and kitchen, and fine broad staircase. The antient domestic chapel is also standing; and the place of the former rows of praying benches is now occupied with ranks of rotund hogsheads filled with delicious cider. The walls are composed of blue stone, evidently a portion of the adjacent dismantled abbey of Newenham; and the beautiful arch forming the cellar door was apparently transported intact therefrom.

Traces of fish-ponds, and my lady's "pleasaunce" garden, may be observed in the adjoining orchard—and a solitary memento of its former attractions, still green and vigorous, yet remains to connect the past and present together, and welcome the curious wayfarer—an espalier—now grown to a large and venerable tree, which, as of old, is in its appointed season, regularly laden with clusters of delicious pippins, right luscious and toothsome.

A knock at the door and a pull at the latch string—"Ah! Good morning, how glad to see you!"—from a kind, motherly benevolent form, but now, alas, gathered in the little churchyard, side by side with her courtly and noted predecessors of this old house. O Death! death! why art thou so cruel—thou ravager of our hearts, thou cold and passionless destroyer—thou remorseless sunderer—

"Of joys that come no more,
Of flowers whose bloom is fled—
Of farewells wept upon the shore,
Of friends estranged or dead.

Of all that now may seem,
To memory's tearful eye,
The vanished beauty of a dream
O'er which we gaze and sigh."

"Here come in and rest yourselves," said the resonant and homely tones of the matron's better half; "for 'twill soon be dinner time," continued our host.

Gladly we accepted the proffered hospitality, together with the indescribable sense of comfort afforded by getting "hot through" in one of the great corners of the immense ingle, which was blazing with a glorious fire. A comfortable meal and a cup of spiced cider, made all things right within, and chewing the cud of contemplation quietly, we summon the celebrated name that has made this house so famous, back from the custody of the past, and bring it to the bar of our thoughts awhile.

What a wonderful phantasmagoria passes in review before our minds eye as we sit and gaze abstractedly into the glowing embers of the grateful fire, and think on the extraordinary career of the celebrated man who drew his first breath beneath this roof.

Of the troublous times at the dawn of the Commonwealth, and his young and gentle mother fleeing before the advance of the surly Roundheads from the house of her husband, in Dorsetshire, to find sanctuary and refuge in her loyal father's house at Ashe—of his birth here amid times ringing with peril and anxiety, a sort of presage of the eventful life he was destined to pass through—of his early infancy spent in this beautiful valley, redolent of sweet flowers, and balmy cows and gentle sheep, nursed in the arms perchance of some woodland Hebe. And then we lose him from these sylvan scenes; and ere he has reached his earliest teens we catch the perfumed atmosphere of the Court, and see his childish limbs enveloped in point lace, doublet, and rapier,—the pretty page of an unfortunate and obstinate Prince—the dishonourer of his sister—from whom he received his first patent of nobility, it may be on the ruins of her virtue—and to whom, in the hour of his adversity he proved a renegade. And then the grime and smoke of grisly war began to loom around; and in his sixteenth year he dons the regal scarlet of the soldier, and then a growing blaze of flame and success brightens on and on, to its fullest splendour. Titles, wealth, and victories wait on the advancing footsteps of the "Handsome Englishman," till all a grateful country has in store for her most fortunate son has been proffered. A Prince of the Empire, a vast domain settled on him, and a palace built for his abode—the victor of a hundred fights, with captive Marshals to swell the train of his prisoners—the babe of Ashe had grown to be a giant among earth's race of heroes. And the "divinity that shapes our ends" strangely protected him, too, amid the hazard of the soldier's life, from injury—for Marlborough was no coward—and his escape at Ramillies pictures up, where a cannon shot took off the head of an officer holding the horse he was mounting. And then the haughty, astute, and intriguing Sarah Jennings, his Duchess, the "dear Mrs. Freeman," of Queen Anne—a woman as remarkable in her way as himself. And then the dark cloud that hung with portentous gloom over his declining years, and the ghastly and mean scandals that fell with mildew and canker on the victor's laurels. And, then last scene of all, the advance of a mightier conqueror than himself, and his out-living the possession of his faculties, and his dying the unconscious possessor of his vast heritage of fame. Thus lived, and thus died, John Churchill, Duke of Marlborough, thought we—born in this house.

And what of the result of this carnage that thus sent him to this pinnacle of fame, to us too, thought we,—or to those who shouted pæans of victory at the time, and loaded him with honours and wealth—those "glorious victories" of Blenheim, Ramillies, Oudenarde, and a score of others, reared on the slaughtered myriads who fell in them?—

"It was the English, Kaspar cried
That put the French to rout,
But what they killed each other for
I could not well make out.
But everybody said quoth he
That 'twas a famous victory.

And everybody praised the Duke
Who such a fight did win,—
But what good came of it at last?
Quoth little Peterkin:
Why that I cannot tell quoth he,
But 'twas a famous victory."

Est il possible, said we to ourselves, looking out of the window at the advancing twilight, and recollecting a witticism uttered by the unfortunate James II., in his bitterest hour of trial, at the expense, we believe, of Marlborough, who finally with the rest deserted his royal patron, and who used to employ this exclamation, as one by one the court favourites seceded. At last Marlborough, then Lord Churchill, started also, and poor James, when he heard of it said with a grim smile, "What! is *Est il possible* gone too!"

At least, if he did not go thus, we must leave this comfortable corner—though we shrink to encounter the keen outpost of the frost king on emerging into the open air. A bright moon throws a flood of radiance down, and all inanimate objects are sparkling with their hoary covering, interspersed with intensely dark shadows, and the constraining coldness we dreaded seems to envelop us instantly as we leave the cosy warm nook,—but hark! what was that soft tone, sounding like a sweet throb through the chill air? Again, ah! 'tis the Colyton curfew. What art thou telling us old bell, as thou bridgest over eight centuries in each measured beat of thy iron tongue?

CURFEW.

Over the moorland and down the glade
Swings the old bell's measured tone,
From the distant tower that stands arrayed
In sheen, by the pale moon thrown;
Peering above the tall trees' dark crest,
As a spirit telling some grave behest.

Through the "longdrawn" silent vale it booms—
Down the churl's low chimney top,
Whose curling smoke, 'mid the dingle's glooms,
As a silver cloud, mounts up;
Round the huge-cornered hearth its faint echoes play,
Till lost mid the cracking fire-blaze gay.

The peasant sits by his inglo side
  With his children at his knee,
He lists to the sound with contented pride,
  For he feels that his home is free!
And he welcomes that ever unvarying chime,
As a friend that tells of his boyhood's time.

The 'squire is feasting within his hall,
  Some honored guests among;
The flagon is passing, and one and all
  Are deep in toast and song;—
A moment they pause, as, in fairy peals,
It's voice through the well-closed shutters steals.

The grim old Norman sleeps in his might,
  Within Caen's cloisters lone,
But his elegy every returning night,
  Is rung in the Curfew tone
By the Saxon churl (never found a slave),
As a warning knell o'er serfdom's grave.

And this is the lesson thou hast in store for us, thou reminiscence of the Conqueror of this fair realm—we who have been dreaming for the past hour of victories won, on that warrior's native soil, by the great soldier born within these walls. Surely, Time, thou art the avenger, thy "whirligig" makes all things even at last—as anon thou puttest thy finger thus upon the boastful lip of Fame.

As we pass out of the farmyard a delicious scent of hay catches the sense from an adjoining cow-byre, and calm, contented breathings, with an occasional rustle of the fragrant provender, fall on the ear as we listen awhile to the comfortable, well-cared for animals within.

Thus even in the midst of thy deepest solitude, O Winter, are we reminded of joys to come—that odorous gale tells us of Summer flowers and balmy hayfields—those peaceful sighs of sunny banks and shady glades; and though now

"The green moss shines with icy glare;
The long grass bends its silken form;
And lovely is the silvery scene
  Where faint the moon-beams smile.

Nature again in Spring's best charms,
Shall rise revived from Winter's grave,
Expand the bursting bud again,
  And bid the flower re-bloom!"

THE FOUNDER

OF

WADHAM.

IT has often occurred to us how singularly rich in historical and traditional associations of every kind almost, is this comparatively out-of-the-way eastern angle of our Shire. Of remote British origin is the remarkable chain of hill fortifications stretching along its boundary, and found at Hochsdun, Musbury, Membury, Hembury, and elsewhere—of Roman, the contested Moridunum at Seaton — of Saxon, the mythical slaughter-ground of Brunenburgh and Athelstan's votive Minster on the Axe—of mediæval fame the grand religious foundations of Ford, Dunkeswell, Newenham, and Ottery St. Mary—of social distinction, the regal-blooded Courtenay's Castle of Colcombe, the Nest of the pious Mohuns of Luppit, the Court of the knightly Brooks at Holditch, the House of the noble Bonvilles at Shute, with divers others.

In direct personal renown it is pre-eminently distinguished as being the birthplace of the great Historian of our county, Sir William Pole—its pains-taking Biographer, John Prince—that chivalric and unfortunate spirit, Raleigh—the successful Marlborough—the weird Coleridge, and a host of others of lesser reputation. To this long list of notabilities we propose now to add the antecedents of another name, which should be justly included among them, and to make record of a visit to the grave of the mother of the munificent Founder of Wadham College, Oxford, and the old home of the family, where he was probably born, at Edge, in Branscombe.

The parish of Branscombe is one of the most romantic and picturesque in the county. The name itself, as chosen by its early colonists, gives a free and comprehensive description of its scenery — *Brans-Combe*—two British words, whose modern equivalent would imply, *the Crow's-dingle*—and there is no better introduction to its attractions than a walk over the hill from the neighbouring village of Beer. As we gain the crest of the hill, which is a very high one, we look down at once into the place.

Facing us first, and somewhat to the left, is the ever beautiful sea (which to-day is intensely blue and calm), revealed in a sort of triangular peep, as the hill-sides run down with sharp obliquity to almost a point at the bottom of the narrow, gorge-like valley, and meet at a strip of white building, where a tall signal post and a dot of red bunting tell us Her Majesty's coast watchmen are domiciled. Directly in front, the cliff line is broken and jagged in a remarkable manner into huge plateaus and ravines, and looks like colossal fortifications raised by some past Cyclopean race. At our feet, far below, is Branscombe proper—a series of deep, narrow, tortuous combes, convoluting round high coniform hills of differing shape :—

"Crags, knolls, and mounds confusedly hurled
The fragments of an earlier world,
And mountains that like giants stand
To sentinel enchanted land."

The villages forming the place are three in number—little nests of houses at the bottom of these valleys, half-a-mile apart, but connected together by the main road of the parish, which runs round the base of one of the hills, with a sort of esplanade appearance, well defined by strings of cottages skirting its margin at intervals. The first of these hamlets contains the parsonage; also a portion of an old manse, with tall gable and quaint gargoyles, and the village "public," the second, the church and one or two antient farm-houses; the third, the village smithy, the ubiquitous preaching-house of the disciples of Wesley, and sundry cottages.

We must now descend from this elevated station, and our path zig-zags down the steep declivity through a copse of stunted trees and thick under-growth. To our right rises a noble rocky hill, at the base of which are the remains of an old unused lime quarry of large size, whose crater, scooped out of the side of the eminence, and serrated at the edges, gives it a sort of volcanic appearance. And, see! one, two, three—down the path with express speed, their long ears laid flat on their shoulders, and little white dossils of tail in the rear, rising and falling in jerky gallop, and now evanished in the brushwood instanter! Plenty of these "feeble folk" here about we surmise, dwelling in "their houses in the rocks" around, with ample range for their teeming families.

This is not a region of flowers exactly, but beautiful patches of the purple-tufted heath fringe the path at intervals; while above rise short growths of the prickly gleaming-leafed holly, interspersed anon with glorious bursts of the thousand-flowered aureous-tinted furze—

> "Each blossom with a troop of swords,
> Drawn to defend it,—"

the faint peculiar odour from which, as we pass, salutes the sense, borne on the wings of the light breeze, that eddies upward from the valley.

A brisk half-hour's walk through the vicarage village, and we halt at the gate of the little churchyard.

"Where can we get the key?" said we to our friend, turning half round and looking toward an open doorway in an antique building close by—

"Here, sir, if you please;" said a venerable but hale figure, emerging from the cottage, and passing his hand over the scattered silver of his brow—"I've been sexton here near sixty years."

The church at Branscombe is a most interesting structure, and one of the oldest in East Devon. The tower is a perfect specimen of early English work; massive in size, with plain parapet, and a serried string course of characteristic corbel heads running round under. The nave is of similar date, character, and ornament, but has received many patchings and meddlings. The chancel and transepts are later additions of the early decorated era, and the east window is a very good example of late perpendicular.

In the chancel are numerous monuments to the families of Bartlett, Bampfield, and others, once resident in the parish; the incised cross moline of an antient vicar in the pavement of the south transept; and a pretentious marble memorial in the nave, to a certain old "Justice Stuckey," who resided at the now dismantled house at Weston, and was a great terror in his day and generation to smugglers, and all other petty ill-doers and offenders against the common peace of those parts.

The object of our visit, the monument of the mother of the Founder of Wadham, is in the north transept; which, however, was not its original place. It was removed to its present situation about forty years ago, from under the window in the south transept, where, without doubt, the lady is interred.

The memorial consists of a pediment (in the centre of which is the *rose* of Wadham), supported on a base rusticated at the sides. On its face, in *alto-relievo*, are—first, two male figures, kneeling on cushions, facing each other, with their hands joined in prayer, and between them is a helmet and pair of gauntlets, evidently intended to belong to the effigy on the right. The figure on the left is attired in a ruff, and an academic or lawyer's gown—that on the right in complete armour, with sword and ruff.

Behind each of these gentlemen is the much smaller figure of a lady, both exactly alike, and evidently meant for the same person. At the rear of the lady, on the left, are fourteen little figures, five boys and nine girls—her children by her first husband; and, again, behind her on the right, are six children—her issue by her second spouse, four boys and two girls.

Below these figures is a black panel, now denuded of its antient inscription; but the ever useful Prince gives a copy of it:—

> "Here lieth intombed the body of a virtuous and antient gentlewoman descended of the antient house of the Plantagenets, sometime of Cornwall, namely, Joan, one of the daughters and heirs unto John Tregarthin, in the county of Cornwall, Esq. She was first married unto John Kelleway, Esq., who had by her much issue; after his death she was married to John Wadham, of Meryfeild, in the county of Somerset, Esq., and by him had (six) children. She lived a virtuous and godly life and died in an honourable age, Sep. :—— in the year of Christ, 1581."

Over the figures are three shields of arms, of which, at the risk of being somewhat dry, we feel inclined to subjoin the bearings, as they relate and confirm substantially the main issue, and make the matter intelligible.

Shield 1—*Baron,* quarterly of four—

1. Two glaziers' irons in saltire, between four pears pendant.—KELLEWAY.
2. A stag's face.
3. A chevron between three escallops.
4. As 1.

Impaling; *Femme,* quarterly of six—

1. A —— ? saltire.—TREGARTHIN.
2. A stag's face.
3. Semee of escallops, a lion rampant.
4. Within a bordure engrailed bezantee, a lion rampant, a label of three.—PLANTAGENET, EARL OF CORNWALL.
5. On a bend five roundles.
6. On a chevron three fleur-de-lis.

This is the achievement of John Kelleway and his wife Joan Tregarthin, and placed over their effigies.

Shield 2—a lozenge quarterly of six, charged the same as *femme* on Shield 1.; being the arms of Joan Tregarthin, an heiress and widow probably to both husbands.

Shield 3—*Baron,* quarterly of nine—

1. A chevron between three roses.—WADHAM.
2. On a chevron three martlets.—CHISELDON.
3. On a chief two stag's faces.—POPHAM.
4. A chevron between seven roundles.
5. Six lioncels rampant.
6. A chief indented, a bend over.
7. Barry, an eagle displayed.—SPEKE ?
8. A lion rampant.
9. A bend fusily.—HEALE.

Impaling; *Femme,* quarterly of six, as on Shield 1;

together forming the coat armour of John Wadham, and his wife Joan Tregarthin (late Kelleway), and placed over their effigies.

The monument was originally fully emblazoned in colours, but has since been repeatedly whitewashed.

Thus the inscription given by Prince is substantially confirmed by the circumstantial sculptured statement still remaining on this remarkable monument, as that commemorating the venerable and twice-widowed Joan Tregarthin, the fruitful mother of twenty children; among which numerous progeny occurs the celebrated name of her son Nicholas, the munificent Founder of Wadham, and who, as his mother is here buried, it is in nowise improbable to believe was born at the old home of the family at Edge, in this parish.

Enough, you will probably say, gentle reader, of this dull genealogical category; and yet thoroughly interesting is it to trace these careful and invaluable displays of the ancient herald's art; for how completely and truly do they establish in their own peculiar language the descent of families when all other record is gone. Thus, think we, as we sit in the corner of a seat and quietly jot down the elaborate armorial display.

But what sweet scent is this we catch faintly at intervals, like a fragrant ghost, roaming at large in this damp and musty corner of the church? A glance at a heap of well-thumbed books in the corner by our side revealed its origin at once. There lay the odoriferous, carefully tied, " Sunday afternoon's nosegay " of some cottage girl—that indispensable *addendum* to the prayer book and snowy handkerchief, left inadvertently the previous day, Sunday.

Ah, ye happy flowers, there is no act of parliament levelled against your sweet priesthood as ye swing your odorous censers, in silent worship, by thousands over hill and dale, in the great temple of Nature, nor to rebuke the gay colours of the vestiture that decks so splendidly your ceaseless ministry.

THE SUNDAY NOSEGAY.

What shall I pluck thee—Phyllis dear,
For this afternoon's nosegay?
What flowers d'ye like best; tell me clear,
To take to church to-day?

A bloody warrior, Robin—take,
Flaming with red and gold!
I love bold hearts that do not quake,
And love that don't grow cold.

What next dear Phyllis?—take thee thyme,
Sweet, useful, lasting, sound;—
I love hard work now in my prime,
And to be handy found.

Also carnations—white and clove,
Just one of each I mean;
Their modest fragrance, Rob, I love,
With all things pure and clean.

Aught else?—why Robin! boys-love, sure,
  Nonsense, I said not rue;
I love—oh who can this endure?
  O Robin! I love—you!

Then take me to the church, my maid,
  Nay—why aside thus start?
Would that I was this nosegay, laid
  For ever o'er thy heart!

A walk round the churchyard of course. What huge oblong stone is this half buried in grass just outside the end of the south transept?

"That's a stone kawfin, zur," said our ancient friend, the sexton—"and they sais he was a brot here vrom Awterton, by some vawk that once lived in theas parish, but I don't mind it."

Very likely not, we thought to ourselves. The ponderous stone—which we would have given a Jew's eye to have seen turned over and noted the interior—in all probability was removed from the church at some distant time; possibly from just inside the transept where Mrs. Joan Wadham's monument originally stood, and where she was doubtless buried—and as the sepulchral stone with the incised cross moline is also on the pavement a little in front of the window, with the abbreviated words,

"Orate pro anima John Hedraunt."

it is in nowise improbable to suppose that this was the said John Hedraunt's coffin—turned out to make way for Mrs. Joan Wadham's last resting place—at least so we surmise.

Here is a vigorous seventeenth century epitaph of a farmer, traditionally said to have died suddenly at a sheep-shearing, found on an old fragment of a tomb-stone :—

"STRONG AND AT LABOUR SUDDENLY HE REELS,
DEATH CAME BEHIND HIM AND STRUCK UP HIS HEELS,
SUCH SUDDEN STROKES SURVIVING MORTALS BID YE,
STAND ON YOUR WATCH, AND BE YE ALSO READY."

Another of similar date, and with characteristic punning allusion to a father and son named Lee buried at "one time, together in one grave :"—

"THE WINE THAT IN THESE EARTHEN VESSELS LAY
THE HAND OF DEATH HAS LATELY DRAWN AWAY,
AND AS A PRESENT SERVED IT UP ON HIGH,
WHILST HEERE THE VESSELS WITH THE LEES DO LYE."

A third tells us of an unfortunate exciseman, "who fell from the cliff between Beer and Seaton as he was extinguishing a fire which was a signal to a smuggling boat."

O Death ! by how many covert ways dost thou lay siege to the defenceless citadel of life.

The ancient and respectable family of Wadham was located for many generations at Edge, between which place and their other seat at Merrifield, near Ilminster, they, says Prince, "resided, sometimes in one, and sometimes in the other, as their inclination led them;

as may appear from their interments in Branscombe Church, whereof we have one example in the mother of Nicholas Wadham, the last of this name, who lies buried there; which may administer to us a probable ground to suppose, that he was born in that parish." Of them was Sir John Wadham, a Justice of the Common Pleas in the reign of Richard II. "He lieth interred most probably in the aisle belonging to the family at Branscombe."

An ancient member of this family is buried under a fine monument in the transept of Ilminster Church. The tomb itself is a very large one, of altar shape, with rows of niches under, while on the top is inlaid in a ponderous slab of Purbeck marble the full length figures of a knight and lady under a rich canopy. The knight is habited in a very early suit of complete plate armour, with basenet and sword—the lady in a cover-chief and long robes. Of the border legend, the following portion only remains:—

> "Simul cujus Willmo Wadhm filio eadem que obiit—die mensis—Anno dni millmo cccc—a qui quidem Willms."

It is a curious example, as the age and dates were never sculptured on the brass, the monument having been probably erected during the lifetime of the knight—a not uncommon occurrence. There is a further rhyming Latin epitaph at the feet of the figures. The shields of arms are unfortunately gone, but a *rose*, the badge of the family, occurs between each word of the ledger line.

Another Wadham finds a resting place in the chancel of the fine old church of Whitchurch-Canonicorum, Dorset—let his epitaph describe who he was :—

> "Here lyeth John Wadham, of Catherston, Esquyer,—who deceased the XIII of Marche in Anno Dni 1584—who was dewring his life time Captayne of the Queenes Maities Castell of Sondesfote besides Weymouth in the Countye of Dorset and also Recorder of Lyme Regis; Whos soule God rest in pese."

The monument is of very late debased Gothic design, and again we are foiled to trace him, as the arms are wrenched out. How often have we experienced this teasing mischief in the loss of the arms, which being small generally, and easily removable, the sacrilegious hands have usually been successful in their thievish designs to make away with them.

Wandering are we in more senses of the word than one; for we have taken flight out of Devon altogether, into the border land of Dorset and Somerset. But we have thought it would be interesting to put on record such an account of the monuments of this reputable family as we remembered having seen, and, as Captain Cuttle says, "made a note of." In furtherance of this view, and even at the risk of being tedious (yet we hope not to be found so), as we have brought the reader to the probable birthplace of the Founder, so ere we conclude we shall take him to the tomb where himself and his wife are sepulchred. But first we must speak of that good wife and her lineage; and finally conclude with a look at the old mansion at Edge.

As Devonshire may with just probability claim the honour of being the Founders' birthplace, so by a rare combination of circumstances she may claim also the further fame of being very "nearly related to that excellent gentlewoman his wife," who with her husband was joint Foundress of the College.

Dorothy Petre, the wife of Nicholas Wadham, was second daughter of the celebrated secretary—Sir William Petre—"to four several Princes,"—another noted Devonian (born at the little parish of Tor-Brian, in South Devon), by his first wife Gertrude Tyrrel, of Warley, in Essex. Secretary Petre lived in an age which to some was fortunate for the easy acquirement of landed property—at the time of the dissolution of religious houses, and his official standing gave him immense advantages, which he fully availed himself of.

Prince gives a not very enviable picture of this statesman's art of serving divers Sovereigns, and of keeping the property he had thus acquired, which rivals in some respects the resolve of the vicar of Bray:—"He had gotten a great estate of abbey lands, but, fearing lest the restoration of the Romish religion by Queen Mary might endanger his enjoyment thereof, he had prudently secured a special dispensation from Pope Paul IV., for the retaining of them, withal affirming he was ready to employ them to spiritual uses." And it appears an immense property, consisting of twelve manors and four rectories, was thus confirmed to him by a bull bearing date 1555, temp: Philip and Mary.

This was only a portion of his great wealth, and we do not find very much returned to their original "spiritual uses" at his hands, except the fellowships and scholarships founded by him at Exeter College, Oxford, and some insignificant charities comparatively in Essex. But in the person of his daughter, Dorothy Wadham, whose fortune, doubtless, consisted of a portion of the spoil, something considerable was so set aside.

Nicholas Wadham, having no issue, after various schemes, settled within himself finally to found a college at Oxford; but, dying before he could complete the work he had designed, left the "whole menagery" of the affair to his wife and some friends in trust, which she and they righteously carried out. Prince further narrates that it was quite a chance after all that the foundation went to Oxford, for "first he thought of founding a college at Venice for such youth of the English nation as, being addicted to the Roman faith and religion, should go in these parts, he and his wife being supposed to be that way inclined." Better counsels intervened, and in the charter of incorporation of Wadham, notwithstanding that "however she and her husband were known to be Popishly affected," it is enjoined "that all their scholars should resort to divine service, as it is now professed."

So, amid the proud coronal of towers that ennobles Oxford, the college of Nicholas and Dorathy Wadham finds its distinctive place :—

"The sweet remembrance of the just
Shall flourish when he sleeps in dust."

But, to continue our narrative, where sleep they in dust? In the transept of Ilminster church, under a stately marble tomb, with their two magnificent effigies in brass let into its spacious marble table. He in complete armour and bare-headed—she in ruff, farthingale, and all the elaborate addenda of costume rife at that period.

Over his head is a label thus inscribed :—

"Death is unto me advantage."

Over hers another, thus :—

"I will not dye, but lyve, and declare ye works of ye Lorde."

At their feet are these inscriptions :—

"Here lyeth interred the body of Nicholas Wadham, whiles he lyved of Merefield, in ye county of

Somersett, Esquier, Ffounder of Wadham Colledge in Oxforde, who departed this lyfe ye XX day of Octob: 1609."

"Here also lyeth ye body of Dorothie Wadham, widdow, late the wife of Nicholas Wadham, Esq., Foundresse of Wadham Colledge in Oxforde, who died the 16th May, 1618, in the yeare of her age 84."

Over them are the arms of Wadham impaling Petre—and between them at the top is a large shield and also a similar one on the pediment of the monument, charged with exactly the same quarterings *baron* and *femme* as the shield No. 3, on the Branscombe tomb; thus clearly identifying the connection of mother and son. Above the shield on the tomb at Ilminster, is the family crest.

There is also a long laudatory poetic Latin epitaph, and another inscription stating that the monument was restored by Thomas Strangeways, Esq., and Sir Edward Wyndham, Baronet, who married the two sisters and heirs of Nicholas Wadham. The Earl of Ilchester, as descendent of the Strangeways, still holds the antient seat and barton of Edge.

Thus, gentle reader, with the arms upon the tomb of Nicholas Wadham, we bring you back to Branscombe again, and now by your leave we will proceed to the old house at Edge. Branscombe is, as we have described, a very picturesque parish, and in one of the most romantic of its many sylvan attractions, the ancient seat of the Wadhams, is situate.

Turning off up a lane to the right, about half-way between the vicarage and church villages, you wind away for about a mile up one of the deep circuitous combes, and there, seated by the side of a hill, a short distance up from the base of the valley, is Edge. All around, the hills are very steep and precipitous; in front is a large copse extending a considerable distance down one side of the valley, at the extreme end of which we catch a small triangular view of the sea.

Of the former habitation of the family very little is left. There is a tolerably perfect gable with a large transomed Tudor window, and the opposite end toward the hill, shews some massive remains of masonry. There is also an old chimney or two, and a circular staircase that formed a portion of the antient building. The original house was apparently a small one, and built probably about the middle of the sixteenth century.

Viewed from the valley below, the windowed gable has rather a fine appearance; and as we were admiring it, a starling mounted on the finial at its apex, his green breast and golden bill glowing in the evening sunlight as he poured out his unmistakable long-drawn whistling wail, soon darting off, however, under the thatched eaves to his speckled wife.

Turning our faces homeward, we bid adieu to the house of Wadham and its olden associations. The sun is getting low, and long shadows stretch down over the grassy acclivity. Over head a few straggling rooks are slowly floating towards their roosting place in the thick shelter of the copse opposite. All is quiet and undisturbed, except now and then the rushing murmur of the breaking tide, rising and swelling on the faint breeze, for the great ocean itself is before us, glowing in the evening sunlight, with here and there a stray sail, some near and others just discernable in the far distance. O glorious, never-tiring sea, the associations of men *may* fail; but thine, garlanded as they are with the eternal imperishable beauty of Nature, never end.

GOOD NIGHT.

Good night!—from a form in shadow
  That meets me in the lane—
From a blythesome farmer's lad, now
  On his homeward road again—
Singing the song of his sweetheart
  At service far away;—
Just two kind words as we meet—part
  The strain of his roundelay.

Good night! from a light step speeding
  Along the pathway lone,
It's terrors all unheeding,
  A low and trustful tone—
Speaks—'mid some soft caresses,
  By anxious lips addressed
To a tiny form, she presses
  Close to a mother's breast.

Good night! and a hale voice greets me
Where sturdy footfalls come,
And a weary labourer meets me,
Seeking his village home;
To his household wee, returning,
Laden with hard earned spoil,
Store for his ingle burning,
Tythe of his long day's toil.

Good night,—from stars that glimmer
Their endless farewells bright—
Good night,—from earth that dimmer
Speaks the adieu of night:
Good night,—from a heart that prayeth
Secret to heaven's throne,
Good night! from ONE who sayeth
Thou never art alone!

JOHN PRINCE

THE

DEVONSHIRE BIOGRAPHER.

A LUSTROUS warm atmosphere, and a changeful sky; emblematic of sweet April, though her glowing elder sister, sunny May, is now verging towards mid-age. Masses of dark humid cloud are slowly passing over the intensely blue void of heaven, and anon scattering their watery arrows with transitory vehemence, between the bright bursts of sunshine. Far down the valley a larger wrack than common curtains out from an adjoining hill crest, and, facing the dark mass, the glowing opalescent half circle of the rainbow attests the fall of of its glittering burthen.

The trees have just put on their new year's suit of leaves, and are quietly waving their branches in the gentle morning breeze, over the polished depths of the river, like a fresh-clothed gallant at his glass:—

> "O thou breeze of Spring!
> Streams have felt the sighing
> Of thy fragrant wing."

Fragrant, aye—for the flowers are everywhere. What would be the aspect of these meadows without them?

by covert banks, over the river, the great golden ranunculus exhibited his exuberant clusters; along the oozy ditches, ranks of bleached lady-smocks trembled on their long stems, while at intervals, a few lingering primroses—

> "Mild offspring of a dark and sullen sire!"

showed their pale starry clusters, and bare sweet company in the hedgerows. The wee daisy was broad awake everywhere, having long since doffed his ruby nightcap and donned his silver frill; his lofty neighbour, the butter-cup, was leisurely unfolding his golden chalice—

> "The bees hummed o'er the level mead,
> Where knots of trembling cowslips bowed;"

and the swallows, a gay company, were bounding and careering around, showing their snowy breasts and jetty backs to the sun-glint.

This was a faint picture of things around, as we sat down on the banks of the Axe, a field, *plus* Bow Bridge, just as the Axminster clock had finished striking the hour of three-fold trine (the chimes in the old tower tinkling away merrily), and were putting together and overhauling our slender fishing "harness" for action.

What fly this morning? A small, tidy palmer, of course, as a stretcher—what beside? We cast a look into the quiet water at our feet—a kind of little bay among some reeds, at the foot of a stickle, where a gentle current flows in and round. Ah! of course, there thou art, thou tiny, delicate sailor, with thy fragile, sail-like wings of transparent steel gauze—the iron blue. A thousand glittering eyes and fleet fins are waiting the advent of thy short life this morning, to make it even shorter, as the continuous quick flips and plunges testify in the adjoining stickle. But stay, we shall endeavour to make reprisals on thy natural enemies this morning.

Now a hunt over our book, and we select an excellent representative, tied by some lissom fingers in the adjoining town. A plague on't! there, at last! after three several tyings and slippings, those "rises" in the river are making us nervous and impatient. One more furred and feathered ambassador, of sallow jaundiced hue and bloated dimensions, with name unmentionable to ears polite, but of special importance in our speckled friends' bill of fare, and our collar is complete. Don't hurry—the whole day is before us—what sound was that?

> "Oh, cuckoo, shall I call thee bird,
> Or but a wandering voice?"

There he comes with hawk-like flight, and has mounted the topmost branch of yonder elm, and is pouring out his glorious fluty diapsons down the vale.

What an indescribable charm do those two soft continuous notes convey to the mind amid the unfolding beauties of sunny spring—the sweet oracle of its hopeful and blissful anticipations and associations.

And now a cast or two into the sparkling river. Gone!—gone again! with a vigorous momentary tug at the slender deception, but with a sharper reminder this time, and, a narrow escape to boot, for our collar has come back festooned in elegant convolutions, which enables us to exhibit five minutes patience in the unravelling. Once more in order, and our extended flight pitches like a snow-flake. There, again! ah! hooked this time, as we surmised from the business character of the rise. Steady—you're a plucky rascal, and in good condition, too, from your strength and resistance, we find—but gently is the word, or the small hook will tear out; there, safely landed, full six ounces avoirdupoise, with a coat of lustrous pearl, dappled over with rubies, and now securely stowed in our wattled creel, with a handful of sweet clover and buttercups for a bier.

Thus with varying success, sometimes landing a fish and sometimes losing one, we saunter quietly down the river half a mile, until the outer signal post of the railway almost vexatiously warns us we are approaching our journey's end. It has been a pleasantly spent hour, though our temper has been somewhat ruffled at intervals, by one of those now numerous fishing novices, or rather nuisances, who, in defiance of all piscatory courtesy, has crossed our fishing ground repeatedly, and from his appearance and cart-load of gear, looked like Behemoth come to swallow up our sweet stream. Even as we reeled up we watched him, two fields in advance, striding along, his arm and rod going like the sail of a windmill—

His luggage half a ton,
His fish an ounce!

Now across a couple of fields, to look at old Newenham Abbey, or rather where it stood; permission being asked and courteously granted by the worthy occupant of the farmhouse, which is built on part of the site.

We were shown into an orchard at the back of the premises.

"And is this all that remains of Newenham Abbey?" asked we, looking at a few massive foundations peeping up amid the green sward, and the ruinous fragment of a thick wall, with indications of arches on one side, which originally formed a portion of the ancient cloister.

"This is all that is left," said he, "except the old chapel yonder," pointing to the decaying walls of a small building, at the end of which was the stonework of a window with beautiful triple lancet openings; while up over, the cherishing ivy had clambered and hung down in dark lustrous masses.

Here stood a noble Abbey, founded early in the thirteenth century by two pious brothers, Sirs William and Reginald de Mohun. A curious little story hangs on the circumstance that made Lady Alice de Mohun, the mother of these two knights, the wife of their father Sir Reginald de Mohun the elder, and is, perhaps, worth the recounting.

There lived in that age a powerful baron having large possessions in Devonshire, Lord Briwere by name, and this nobleman had a pious and dutiful daughter called Alice. It would seem that Reginald de Mohun, her subsequent spouse, was left an orphan while but a child, and as he had a great property bequeathed to him, the wardship of the parentless boy was eagerly sought after—as according to a monstrous law of that age, the territorial property, personal liberty, and matrimonial prospects of a ward, were almost absolutely at the disposal of his trustee.

This privilege of thus taking care of the young Reginald, was accorded by the King, Henry III., to Lord Briwere, who, with proper regard to family interests, in due time married the youth to his fair daughter Alice; and as both the young people were of distinguished birth, and had large inheritances, we may conclude that the matrimonial arrangements terminated happily. The whimpled and robed effigy of this lady, clasping the blessed Virgin and Child to her breast, is found in the chancel at Axminster.

The "nest" of this noble family was at Mohun's Ottery, and our readers will doubtless recollect the description of our visit to the old place. To-day we are about to explore a munificent foundation, the offspring of their pious beneficence—a splendid example of real, tangible, self-denying religious faith, however imperfectly set forth, contrasted with the starved sentimentality of the present day.

We must now invite the reader to carry his thoughts backward some three centuries, and imagine to himself a magnificent Church and Conventual buildings standing on the site indicated by the faint traces of foundations now visible along the green turf.

The Abbey-Church itself was a splendid building, about three hundred feet long by one hundred and fifty wide, with a lofty tower, built in the early English or lancet style, contemporary with Salisbury Cathedral, and designed probably by the same architect, as the names of both are very similar, and Lady Alice de Mohun, the mother of the Founders of this structure, also gave a large portion of the stone used for the erection of that Cathedral.

The Church was dedicated to the Blessed Virgin on the 6th of July, 1250.

The whole has passed away, Conventual buildings and all, where, for more than three hundred years, twenty-six successive Abbots and their reverend brotherhood lived in peaceful contemplation and retirement.

NEWENHAM.

Abbey of Newenham! and is this all
That now remains to speak thy olden fame?
These mouldering relics of a broken wall,
Marking the spot still hallowed by thy name.

How altered now, from when thy structure rose,
Amid the trees in quiet stately grace,
When all around thee breathed a calm repose,
And thou in this fair valley kept thy place.

When knight and noble at thy shrines oft bowed,
And rich oblations proved a wealthy store,
When belted barons at thy altars bowed,
And ever faithful to thy interest swore!

Now gone is altar, arch, and tower, and aisle,
And lost the saint in fretted niche enshrined,
Buttress and battlement, and all that style
And art and beauty once had here combined.

Gone too the solemn choir, where eve and morn,
The grave procession slowly wound along,
While rising to the vaulted roof was borne,
The holy strain of chant and sacred song.

And cloister dim, where oft the sandalled feet
Of grey cowled monk pass'd on with measured tread,
When meditation made the dull hours sweet,
And pious thoughts had worldly visions sped.

And all that would have told that these had been,
Save here and there an o'ergrown ridge of stone,
For e'en the deep foundation scarce is seen,
So sure hath Ruin reared her crumbling throne.

But Solitude hath wove her charm around,
And Legend cherishes the hallowed spot,
While Fancy revels freely o'er the ground,
And pictures to herself these scenes forgot.

We must not forget to notice a remarkable incident

as having occurred in the otherwise unruffled annals of Newenham, and the consequent flutter of surprise and preparation that filled the breast of a certain good Abbot, John, and his fraternity, on a murky November morning, in the year of grace, 1497. On that occasion the parsimonious and learned Henry VII., visited the Abbey, on his return from Exeter, after the suppression of Perkin Warbeck's rebellion, journeying hither from Ottery St. Mary.

The King appears to have remained several days, and to have gone over to Shute, where lived my Lord Bonville, Marquess of Dorset—a nobleman high in his Grace's estimation—to enjoy the sport of archery at the Butts there; but the Royal traveller does not appear to have been very successful as a bowman, as mention is made in the Privy Purse expenses of the time of sundry sums, and a valuable ring of gold, "lost at the butts to my lord marques."

Hush! we are on holy ground. Beneath this green turf reposes the dust of hundreds. Within those dimly descried foundations lies many a noble scion of the families of Mohun and Bonville—the first Founders of the Abbey, and their descendants, together with all the succession of reverend Abbots, there from time to time deposited "in His faith and fear."

"The whole breadth of the choir," says Mr. Davidson, "was occupied by a series of interments disposed in regular order. Of these, the first on the south side of the altar against the wall, and near the seats of the ministers, was the body of Sir Giles de Cancellis, the donor of Plenynt to the Abbey; next him lay Sir William de Mohun, one of the Founders, and then his brother, Sir Reginald, whose remains occupied a spot near the officiating deacons station. Close to his father, under a small stone, was deposited the heart of Sir John de Mohun, whose body was buried at Bruton; and next to it the remains of Sir William de Mohun of Ottery-Mohun, his half brother: lastly, against the north wall of the choir, lay Sir Nicholas Bonville, a benefactor to the Abbey, who died in 1266. The bodies of several other individuals of the Bonville family were buried in the nave, and in the centre of the choir between them and the high altar, immediately before the great cross, lay the remains of the wealthy and munificent Sir William Bonville of Shute, who died 1407, and those of Alice his second wife."

Without the church a host of sleepers are sepulchred —the cowled brethren of the cloister, together with all those who dwelt within the Abbey precinct, and for three hundred years were gathered one by one into the silent fold of death under the shadow of her walls.

What a spectacle of wondrous awe would be presented, we contemplatively and reverently picture to ourselves, if that voice of the Omnipotent that originally called them into being, were now to summon the inanimate dust back once more to His presence! The earth under our feet would spring to life, and the enclosure itself scarcely yield sufficient room for the awakened sleepers to appear on. And yet the time will surely come when this dread scene will be called into being—when that multitude which no man may number, shall awake at the sound of the last trump, and the earth and the sea give up their dead, summoned by that Voice which alone can

"Back to its mansion call the fleeting breath!"

Thus, with sobered musings, we stealthily and slowly pace round, and explore the enclosure. The apple trees that take root in the hallowed soil seem like mute and loving mourners, keeping continuous watch and ward over the entombed host below. At present their branches are all a-blush with sweet blossoms, through which the bees are keeping a continuous hum, and the ground beneath is strewn with the fallen, pale, odorous petals.

But gracious Heaven! what see we there! starting back, as our eyes unconsciously wandered among the branches of a short apple tree, at the further extremity of the enclosure. A grinning, chapless, human skull, perched on a large limb, but evidently placed there from motives of safety and care, was staring vacantly at us through a kind of screen of lesser boughs, loaded with pink bloom. Peace! thou bounding heart—the unexpected sight of that cavernous arch and those eyeless sockets has disturbed the regularity of thy "healthful music" sadly, as the misgiving crosses thee that to this complexion we also must come some day.

Who was this, thought we, taking the mouldering relic down from the branch—not an old man evidently from the regularity of the teeth, and one of good power of mind, judging phrenologically by the ample development of the frontal portion of the skull—one of the monks probably.

The place of his sepulchre was soon found. A little brook—that originally ran outside the Abbey precinct and doubtless supplied the fraternity with its ample supply, swollen with some late rains, had fretted through the corner of the hedge into what was apparently the common graveyard of the monastery—was the unconscious exhumer, for a portion of the bank had fallen, and there the extended skeleton of the monk, stretched in his last long sleep, was easily traceable, about four feet below the surface.

The skull was placed in the branch for security, and was afterwards re-buried, with the skeleton—and the stream turned back to its original channel.

> "Who sleeps below! who sleeps below?
> It is a question idle all;
> Ask of the breezes as they blow,
> Say, do they heed, or hear thy call?
> They murmur in the trees around,
> And mock thy voice, an empty sound.
>
> Then what is life, when thus we see
> No trace remain of life's career?
> Mortal! whoe'er thou art, for thee
> A moral lesson liveth here;
> Place not on aught of earth thy trust,
> 'Tis doomed that dust shall mix with dust.

What doth it matter then, if thus
  Without a stone, without a name,
To impotently herald us—
  We float not on the breath of fame,
But, like the dew drop from the flower,
Pass after glittering for an hour,
Or, a ripe apple falling down
Unshaken 'mid the orchard brown!"

An old and oft told tale. Perhaps he was one of the victims of the ghastly plague that ravaged the Abbey during the rule of Abbot de la Houe, about the middle of the 14th century, when every soul living here was swept away, except that reverend dignitary and two of the monks! What an awful season of trial must that have been. Or did he waste silently and almost imperceptibly away in his little cell—like a beauteous flower carefully tended and nourished, but slowly and surely perishing in tint and odour, till death put his irrevocable but hallowed seal upon his brow, and the mournful requiem chanted its sadly exultant strain over his bier, as an earth-freed spirit now translated with the blest. But who may penetrate the mystery of thy secret, O grave?

There is another association connected with these ruins to which we must now recur, and a singularly appropriate association it is. Here was born in 1643, the celebrated biographical chronicler of our Shire, John Prince, the learned, chatty, pains-taking author of the *Worthies of Devon,* among whose long list of notabilities he himself now occupies a distinguished place. His father was Bernard Prince, of Newenham Abbey, and his mother Maria Crocker, of Lyneham. Subsequently his father married Jane, daughter of Philip Drake, of Dunscombe, Salcombe Regis, a branch of the Drake family, of Trill, near Newenham, the head of which house then living, Sir John Drake, Prince informs us, was his "honourable god-father."

John Prince, having finished the usual course at Brasenose College, Oxford, took holy orders, and after serving in his vocation as curate, successively at Bideford and St. Martin's, Exeter, was preferred to the living of Totnes; and finally, through the friendship of the Seymours, to the vicarage of Berry Pomeroy, where he ministered forty-two years, dying in 1723, aged eighty, and was there buried, and a small tablet is erected in that church to his memory.

In addition to his *Worthies*, Prince was also the author of several tracts and sermons. His fame, however, rests on his great biographical tome, now a recognised and most valuable county work, full of interesting details, anecdotes and pedigrees; in this latter particular it is especially trustworthy, being derived in great measure from the writer's access to the invaluable store-house of information collected by Sir William Pole. The first edition of the *Worthies* was published in 1701; a second and much improved one, in 1810. A century and half has now elapsed since the original advent of the work, and another biographer is now needed to continue the list of eminent men who have distinguished themselves in the various walks of art, science, discovery, theology, and warlike operations, having been natives of this county, for their name is Legion.

Of our author himself, and his "no less profitable than pleasant and delightful" labours, we cannot do better than conclude with a stanza addressed to him by a contemporary, William Pearse, Vicar of Dean Prior:—

"You've done the work, sir; but you can't be pay'd,
Until among those Worthies you are laid;
Then future ages will unjustly do,
To write of worthies, and to leave out you."

There is yet one more name inseparably connected with these ruins—a most careful, erudite, and correct antiquary, the historian of the Abbey and neighbourhood, the late James Davidson, of Secktor, Axminster. From his retiring disposition few are acquainted with the immense store of most valuable information descriptive of our county he had accumulated after years of the most laborious research, wherein he spared neither time nor expense, every word of which ought to be published; and his magnificent and unequalled library of books relative to the county, the result of a lifetime's discriminating and zealous collection, it is fervently hoped may some day be placed among the most valuable public treasures of our Shire.

Urbane and courteous to all inquirers, the writer of these desultory lines feels the keenest pleasure in recording his obligations of access to Mr. Davidson's resources, and personal friendship and encouragement afforded in the pursuit of little antiquarian inquiries around the neighbourhood. Peace to his ashes—the flower-spread sod of this beautiful valley now forms his perennial winding sheet, like it does those of the good Abbots beneath our feet, the peaceful tenour of whose lives he delighted to chronicle. Both are now resting in the same hope, and awaiting the same blest awakening voice.

A cup of the cheering brown infusion, a great crisp, home-baked loaf, with a basin of cream—such cream! —to be eaten thereon, *ad libitum*, and half-an-hour's chat with our host. As we enjoyed the dainty rural spread, we queried to ourselves as we looked at the massive wall of the house, which was a portion of the old Abbey, whether this was a part of the Refectory, and if so, whether the genial old Abbots on their feast days were ever initiated into the mystery of the glorious delicacy we were now enjoying; not the tea assuredly—(though not the least so to us, now)—but the cream, with the thirst-inspiring *addendum* probably of mulled wine or spiced ale. If so, they had a right noble, and "dainty dish," fit in every sense to "set before a King," even such as the miserable seventh Henry himself, who once came here, and was comforted by hospitable entertainment, let us hope.

What a picture would be revealed could we draw the veil of time aside, and for an instant get a glimpse of the assembled banqueters—the good Abbot and his fraternity, the King and his retinue, together with all the great nobles of the district, gathered round the table and enjoying themselves with staid decorum and decorous jollity, as befitted the reverend host and his Royal guest. But both King and Abbot are turned to dust, and of the place of their rejoicing scarce one stone remains upon another.

> "Even such is time, that takes in trust,
> Ourselves, our joys, and all we have,
> And pays us only with the dust,
> In the deep coffers of the grave!"

And so, with thoughts such as these, ere we leave, we go out and take a final saunter among the ruins. Another day is nearly gone, for the shadows are lengthening fast, and the sun, matchless monarch of the day, is retreating, with a dignity of glorious splendour, behind the heights of Hampton opposite, defining the dark fringe-like edge of trees down the hill-slope with marvellous distinctness. Oh, glorious sunset, how often hast thou similarly gladdened the eyes of the sleepers below, thou that art now pouring thy flickering gold over the green pall that shrouds their inanimate forms.

Our kind host shewed us some capitals of early English style, found at a considerable depth underground, and informed us that the stone-work of the pillars that supported them when discovered, lay "like a pile of cheese turned over," for regularity—also some fragments of encaustic tiles and bits of painted glass, of which we craved sundry pieces by way of memento. And then we bade adieu to the venerable precincts of Newenham—for the "busy, busy bee," with homeward hum, darted past our ear, and the quick-winged bat was threading his agile flight just overhead.

Off across the meadows once more for half an hour's quiet evening fishing on our road home. We re-adjust our collar, and having placed the captivating white moth among our trio of seeming fly dainties, are soon rewarded by a brace or so of spankers, whose appearance in our basket makes the size and weight of our "dish" respectable.

TROUTING AT EVENTIDE.

INSCRIBED TO "PISCATOR." *

When summer days are in their prime,
  Just in the twilight grey,
I love, adown, at evening time,
  The river's banks to stray.

Rod on my shoulder, at my back
  An osier creel light swung,
Blithesome my tread along the track
  With reed and bulrush hung.

* A right good fisherman, poet, and litterateur, both on the gentle craft, and also the genial and correct historian of the sparkling Axe—with whose well-known pleasant "Book" thereon, the reader (if he has not seen it) is advised to make a speedy acquaintance.

The balmy scent that fills the air,
At every step I meet,
The fragrance rich of flowers rare
And new-mown hay so sweet.

The throstle's good night note I hear,
From out the brook-side brake,
And at the stile, the broad mead near,
The land-rail's busy crake.

The mazy rout of flies are gone,
That thronged the river's brim,
All save the gnats that gambol lone
Within the gap-way dim.

The headlong beetle, whirring round,
Starts from his "shard-born" bed
The white moth flutters from the ground.
Before my stealthy tread.

I linger near an alder's shade,
Where halts the flashing brook,
To form, encircled by the glade,
A pool within a nook;—

A pool, so still no ripple heaves
Across its mirrored face;—
There, 'neath a pollard's spreading leaves,
I take my chosen place.

And watch where soft the evening light
Strikes o'er yon reed clad ledge,
A circle breaks its surface bright,
And quivers to its edge.

With well poised rod, my flimsy gear
Above my head I throw,
And bring it o'er that circle clear
Like flake of falling snow.

A short quick leap, a plunge, a rush,—
My trusty rod bends free;
Swift to his hover 'neath the bush,
With arrow's speed, darts he!

Another rush, as checked from thence
He seeks the nearer shore,
And shows, with brave unyielding fence,
The battle is not o'er.

Undaunted, still with failing strength,
He dares his foe to meet,
Till (such is fate), a prize, at length,
He's lying at my feet.

The speckled brigand of the stream,
Moulded with beauty's line,
Rich o'er his breast of golden gleam
The rays of Iris shine!

Safe landed, others quickly grace
My pannier's filling store,
Till, at the close, three goodly brace
I own, and sometimes more.

Homeward I bend my steps, on high
The stars stud eve's dusk floor;—
The old tower looms against the sky,
And my foot is at my door!

TOPLADY

AND HIS

DEVONSHIRE HOME.

WHO is there among us does not feel his heart a-glow, and his pulse beat a little the faster, at the mention of anything relative to the locality where Augustus Montague Toplady lived and ministered? That daring prophetic spirit, who seems to the mental vision sitting at the feet of Calvin, eagle-winged and firm of purpose, and outstripping the great apostle of his faith even in the positive utterances of his assurance, yet withal clothed in the bright mantle of one of the sweet harpers of Paradise, with his seraph's lyre at his side. Strange admixture of poesy and dogma, yet ever beautiful and ever truthful triumph of love and song. The soft eternal halo of the Poet has long outshone the fiercer glory of the stern Divine, but the piercing rays of conviction that distinguish Toplady in the latter character, have given to his productions the true Promethean incandescence of immortality.

There are doubtless, many people who read the beautiful lyrics of Toplady—see his name on the pages of their hymn books as the sing them on the returning Sabbaths;—say to themselves in their quiet moments stray verses, or repeat one of those inimitable single lines, when their hearts are full or cares infest them, to their exceeding comfort;—with a quiet wonderment who the gifted author was that thus comes to them so nearly in their inner experience, but have never troubled themselves further about his history.

Toplady was a voluminous writer, unsparing and pugnacious, on the congenial absorbing topic of his life—polemical theology, and a bitter wordy warfare was carried on between him and another honoured labourer in the Master's Vineyard—John Wesley. With strange parallelism in development of mind, too, Wesley, like his literary opponent, was one of the sweet singers of Israel; and there is little doubt, now that the "veil darkly" is removed, through which their eager glances stretched to catch closer glimpses of the truth on earth, both of them, from this world's disputations free, are raising as with one voice the beatific hymn of the Redeemed.

Amid the galaxy of poets that bespangle the theological firmament, Toplady must ever take rank as a star of the very first magnitude, and in some respects the glitter of his genius is altogether unapproachable. There is a heartiness, a fervour, a brilliance, and an unquestioning faith in the truth of what he is singing about, that influences the reader with a powerful and riveting charm, which he cannot shake off, even though he be not inclined exactly to follow and acquiesce in the views so beautifully set forth.

A deal of the strength of Toplady resides in the concentration of idea, often expressed in a single line, which for aptness of descriptive power rarely leaves anything more to be said on the thought propounded, and is unrivalled in its peculiar walk of religious song. His lines fall on the ear with unconscious strength, but re-wake afterwards in the memory with surprising freshness and vigour. A study of his poetry in this particular will amply repay the investigator, and give him possibly much of an unrealized view of the capabilities of its author.

With all these special beauties, there is yet perhaps one more which lends even a rarer charm, and enhances the whole of the foregoing; the unquestionable desire of not writing for earthly fame. No trace of vanity for, nor courting of this world's applause, pervades a single stanza, or seeks to lay itself out for it. The hymns are the outpourings of a heart—written *to* man but *for* God. And there is a fragrance and sanctity about them that seems to fully realize the idea embodied in one of our most popular modern hymns:—

"O Paradise,—
Patience, I almost think I hear
Faint fragments of thy song!"

A truce, however, to a bewitching subject—as the main object of this paper is a description of Toplady's

Devonshire home, and the scene of his parochial ministrations.

As the traveller spins along on his way from the clean little market town of Honiton, on the railway, through the long sylvan valley to Exeter, a few miles west of the former place, he will observe on his right a high pyramidal hill, on the top of which are apparent, even from the railway as he passes, the huge earthworks of a large entrenched camp, forming one link of a chain of hill fortifications, that protected the border land of the ancient Danmonii — the olden blue-painted warriors of this merry shire—from their predatory neighbours, the Duotriges of Dorset.

This is Hembury Fort hill, and at the foot of the eminence, securely nestled in another vale, which runs at right angles from the line of railway, is Broadhembury, the country cure of Toplady, to which place he was inducted in 1768. Thus much for the locality by rail; our visit will be by a chaise drive from Honiton, four miles distant.

The road to Broadhembury winds away through an umbrageous lane, nearly up to the apex of the fortress-crowned hill, visible from the railway, and we halt for a few moments on the summit to enjoy the beautiful prospect. The view from this point is magnificent; westward the fertile valley of Honiton extends down to Exeter, fourteen miles distant, behind which rises the mountainous Dartmoor hills, forming a massive barrier against the far-off cloud-land. Below and around the green combes and woody glens lie extended over a vast circuit, as in a map, and the tourist is led involuntarily to admire the excellent situations for look-out, chosen by the ancient British chieftains for their mountain fastnesses.

An easier descent on the other side, for a couple of miles, brings us to the Grange, a fine old mansion in which has resided for generations the Squires of Toplady's parish, the progenitor of whom was a noted law officer to the energetic Virgin Queen. A few hundred yards of farther progress through the devious lane, and the fine old tower, with the conglomeration of thatched roofs at its base, and guarded as it were, by some luxuriant elms, all so characteristic of a Devonian hamlet, and the village of Broadhembury is before us.

There is little more noteworthy than ordinary in the aspect of the place, compared with other west country parishes. The main street is, however, very broad and clean, and the cob-walls, neat thatching, and gay flower-plots in front, give a warm and comfortable appearance to the cottages, and shew that the Squire of the parish is not insensible to the wants and well-being of the peasantry who reside within. A long dairy-string of red Devon cows (for all seems red here, cattle, soil, and houses), are slowly marching home to the evening milking; behind loiters a happy-faced lad and his sworn chum, a great grey-coated, tail-less sheep dog, and both of them are eyeing with great interest the strangers in the little vehicle creeping along by their side.

Making our way onwards toward the swing sign that denotes the village hostelry; we drive in under an antiquated gateway to the yard in the rear. The obliging proprietress, whose husband seems to combine the avocations of farmer and publican, ushered us through several large rooms into the special parlour for strangers, and soon sets before us a dainty spread of sparkling cider, a huge home-made loaf, and a roll of sweet butter, the whole evidently manufactured on the premises.

But a glance round the room itself affords the greatest treat. Its dimensions are small, but the walls, from floor to ceiling, are wainscotted with multitudinous panels of oak, carved into the well known linen pattern, so much used during the reigns of the 7th and 8th Henries, and a rich cornice of boldly carved masks and allegorical devices, runs round at the top. A large stone window, consisting of a series of narrow Tudor arched openings, throws a subdued light into the quaint old apartment, which is a portion evidently of one of those old decayed village manses so numerous in the west of England.

On emerging from the front door of the inn, our attention is at once arrested by a short, wide street, which stretches up a gentle ascent from the main thoroughfare, at the top of which stands the really noble church tower, lofty and pinnacled. This is the attractive feature of the place, and anything finer of its sort is rarely found. Lofty trees, with a stray house or two between, occur on each side, and directly in the centre rises the tower, with a neat wall at its base, fringed over with the usual garnishing of tombstones that peep above the coping.

Quite enjoying the unexpected treat of so pretty an incident, we slowly wend up the acclivity, stopping for a moment at the yard gate to scan the outside of the building. The church is built in what is termed by architects the third pointed or perpendicular style of Christian architecture, and the date of its erection is about the period when so many of our Devonshire sanctuaries were re-built.

The tower is lofty and well proportioned, also the porch, over which are three richly fretted niches, long since denuded of their inhabitants, and a singularly beautiful aisle window at its side attracts notice, with the curiously carved corbel heads, which are attired in the queer horned head dress, so fashionable about the middle of the fifteenth century.

The civil sextoness has by this time arrived, and as the key grates in the lock of the ponderous door, it is with feelings of subdued curiosity, not unmixed with a more than common awe, that we cross the porch threshold. Inside (alas for the rage for modern renovations) the church has been modernised and re-seated, but the restorations have been carefully and judiciously carried out.

The interior probably wears little of the aspect now that it did when Toplady ministered within its precincts, and with the exception of the cunningly carved screen and quaintly painted west gallery, all is probably of modern erection, but taken altogether it is a fine, airy country church.

The usual small gratuity to our homely cicerone, and a request to be left alone to look round the church for half an hour, soon produces the desired effect; depositing the great bunch of keys in our hand with a request for us to put them in at the cottage door at the end of the lane when we have finished our visit, she vanishes through the little side chancel door with a respectful curtsey.

"Alone," we said to ourself, "and in Toplady's church," as we sat down in the corner of a seat, harnessing the twin steeds of meditation and fancy to the car of our thoughts, and giving ourselves freely up to the grand associations of the place and moment.

Here ministered Toplady, these walls have been made eloquent with his voice; here it is justly probable, while setting forth the mystery of his Master's will, the bright glance of the Ineffable broke in upon his heart with living light, and tipped his pen with immortal fire, leaving its record behind in the grandest religious lyric in the English language:—

"Rock of ages, cleft for me!"

We thought of the parallel of two names (do not

be startled gentle reader) of Toplady and Napoleon, of Broad Hembury and St. Helena; the parallel of the masters they served, and respectively of their deeds and of their fame.

Far out in the trackless solitude of the ocean, chained to a rock, and expatriated from the ken of his fellow men, lived and died one, with a reputation for gigantic earthly ambition and its successful grasping such as the world had never seen.

Thousands of his brethren had shed their life blood in stifling death agonies, and had gone down to unknown, unwept, unhonoured, unsoothed graves, to build that reputation up—a reputation founded on the dying curse, the writhing groan, the shriek, the wail, the frightful din and cruelty, of the battle field, the tear of the orphan, the broken heart of the widow.

Such was the purpled Emperor of St. Helena; such the fame, seethed in blood, of the prisoned arch-vulture of king-dom. He served his earthly Master well, and has had his reward.

Here, in his woodland home, a sunny Devonshire valley,

"Far from the madding crowd's ignoble strife"

lived another soldier, patiently and obscurely fighting in another great battle field,

"The world forgetting by the world forgot;"

who carried in his hand not a sceptre but a torch, not a sword but a pen—the torch glowing with the fire of faith and immortality, the pen inscribing the words peace and love.

No ruthless unholy hand of man was needed to manacle him to a solitary rock in the distant void of ocean; another Hand had ordered his goings and set his feet upon the Rock of Ages, that sure fastness of his soul, of which he so sweetly sung. No crowd of captive kings thronged the ante-chambers of his earthly courts, but celestial visitants delighted to wait on him instead.

His fame, too, is built upon the dying hours of men, passing away upon a battle field large as the world itself, where the victory tells of Christ. Millions of dying lips, from zone to zone, from king to peasant, far as the English language is spoken, and in many another tongue, have ceased breathing while whispering his words for their comfort, in quenchless faith, and have carried the faint echo of their assurance direct into the Master's presence. Myriads yet unborn will do the same to the end of time, repeating and still repeating the peerless story of the "Rock of Ages," (which its author with quiet humbleness says, "may be used living or dying,") the ascription of prayer, the burst of praise, the glow of comfort, the beam of peace, the stay and surety of widowed and fatherless.

Such is the white-robed saint of Broadhembury; such the fame of the meek disciple of His Kingdom, who served his heavenly Master well, and hath his reward, dwelling now with Cherubin and Seraphin! Where is the comparison of fame? Our own sweet poet Laureate shall reply:—

> "Wide as this earthly taper's spark
> Is from yon argent round."

Our reverie over, a saunter round the little churchyard completes our visit.

We carefully scan the names commemorated on the tables of stone, those index fingers of the dusty hand of death that point the certain road on which all living flesh is fast hurrying. Several meet our view inscribed with a date, indicating that the now "dull cold ear" of the sleeper below, was doubtless in life privileged to listen to the searching enquiries and dauntless answers of the then unknown but now famous village pastor, let us hope to the auditor's profit and edification.

Toplady's parochial ministry appears to have been no idle vocation, if we may judge from his diary and correspondence. The three last years of life, however, seem to have been passed in London, where he was engaged in a vigorous warfare of enunciating and enforcing his own peculiar opinions. Ill health soon overtook him, and at the age of thirty-eight—an age so fatal to genius—he died, in the full assurance of the faith he had professed during life, and was buried in Tottenham Court Chapel, London.

Once more our thoughts gather round the poetic charms of Toplady, as we call to mind sundry portions of his works. Surprisingly beautiful and complete is his imagery, whether mounting on the fervid fiery pinions of religious exultation and assurance of the future, or hovering and poising in sweet abstraction over some delightfully happy picture of earth born joy. With the real hand of genius he grasps and displays the full embodiment of metaphor or sentiment in a short sentence of wondrous completeness and power, that never requires afterthought to brighten or expand—whether soaring in highest adoration—

"Fountain of never ceasing grace,
Thy saints exhaustless theme,
Great object of immortal praise
Essentially supreme;
All Thy works Thy goodness shew
Centre of perfection Thou!"

or moving in blissful contemplation,

"Lord, it is not life to live,
If Thy presence Thou deny;
Lord, if thou Thy presence give
'Tis no longer death to die;—
Source and Giver of repose
Singly from Thy smile it flows."

describing the beauty of creation,

"The heaven Thy glorious impress wears,
Thy image glitters in the stars;—
The firmament, Thy high abode
Seems too the spangled robe of God.

Whene'er it's beauty I admire,
It's radiant globes direct me higher,
In silent praise they point to Thee,
All light, all eye, all majesty!"

picturing life's probation,

"At anchor laid remote from home
Toiling I cry—sweet Spirit, come
Celestial breeze no longer stay
But swell my sails and speed my way."

or with holy serenity awaiting its trials and close;—

"In suffering, be Thy love my peace,
In weakness, be Thy love my power;
And when the storms of life shall cease,
Jesus,—in that important hour,
In death as life, be Thou my Guide
And save me, Who for me hast died."

We depart from the village in chastened mood, though not altogether untempered with joy. A beautiful setting sun glints warm, lustrous rays through the hedge row bushes, and dapples the lane with oases of shifting splendour, and the massive frontal of Hembury Fort cuts keenly into the grey luminous depth behind it. All is hallowed and peaceful around, scarcely a sound breaks the silence, except the indistinct murmur at intervals of a railway train threading its way down the valley.

What is there for thee, my heart, beyond this earthly beauty and peace—this suffusing splendour above and around? this capacity to understand, to enjoy, and be thankful? Only that place of which our sweet poet had experienced so ample a foretaste; where, without doubt, he is now translated, and become in verity what in life he wished to be,

> "Like the rapt seraph that adores and burns;"

and where, to use his own prophetic words,

> "Thy worship no interval knows,
> Their fervour is still on the wing."

Even there, O heart!

THE GREAT HOUSE, COLYTON,

AND

WHO LIVED THERE.

IF the traveller wishes to see one of the sweetest and most genuine bits of Devonian scenery, to be found within the leafy boundary of our beautiful county, commend him to a look from the railway platform at the little Colyton town station. There before him lies the quaint old-fashioned, thatched-roofed little town, literally embosomed amid luxuriant foliage, with its glorious church tower rising in stately grandeur from its midst. Three or four rich valleys, clad with the greenest verdure, meet at his feet, and the hill slopes around are thickly divisioned with devious-lined hedges, from which spring multitudes of tall elms and the shorter round-foliaged oak, while here and there below from the underlying meadows a few well contrasted spiry poplars shoot up amid the umbrageous mass. Large dim coloured patches of orchard spread themselves at intervals, while on the distant hill lines around, long strips of fir plantations are extended in dark masses against the sky. In the meadows below the sparkling Coly flashes along, as it speeds away from the large, dark, slow moving mill-wheel in the foreground, and the accompanying foaming weir, over which its spare strength sparkles and tumbles.

Having surveyed to our fill this almost unrivalled bit of rural beauty, we descend from the slightly elevated position of the railway station, and turning short round on our left, take our path over the two meadows that lie between us and Colyton.

There is not much to arrest the attention during our short transit over the green turf, nevertheless a large dairy of fine red Devon cows, some leisurely grazing in the meadows and others quietly standing and chewing the cud of contentment in mid-stream of the babbling river, give pleasure to the eye—and a knot of rustic children are settled on the river bank, three or four stretched at full length in listless ease, and as many more sat down by their side twisting posys of the beautiful purple flags, which are now in full blow, and display their rich masses of flowers at intervals along the rivulets' margin.

There, too, rises a noble heron some hundred yards off, from an oozy ditch beyond the adjoining hedge, where he has been patiently standing, possibly, for hours, waiting, like Mr. Micawber, for something to turn up for his dinner—how measured is the beat of his great blue wings, as he leisurely makes his way down the valley.

Arrived in Colyton, there is little to note in its

maze of short streets, except the grand old church, and the adjacent tall-gabled, ivy-clad, free school-house. Threading our way onward, we ask for the lower Seaton road, and there, just as we turn the corner at the top of the town, a fine old hooded elliptic archway meets the eye, with a wing wall, composed of squared black flints of large size, laid in regular tiers, marvellous in appearance, and for the amount of patient labour expended in its construction.

Over this wall an array of Tudor chimneys and windows, and intervening gables, surmounted by Elizabethan finials, make their appearance, and the original residence of the once opulent and powerful, but now extinct, family of the Yonges, Baronets, is before us, the two last representatives of whom were successively Secretaries at War—the one during the early part of the reign "when George the III. was King," and the other to that monarch's father.

Of this now well nigh forgotten race, of themselves, their antient house, their last resting place, and other histories anent, we propose, by your leave, gentle reader, to gossip awhile.

Descended from a certain John Yonge, who was a justice of the Common Pleas in the reign of Edward IV., one John Yonge, gentleman, settled at Colyton (having also a residence at Axminster), about the middle of the sixteenth century. He was an opulent "merchant adventurer" of that era, which seems to have laid the foundation of our present taste and success in commercial prosperity, and was associated with others in a patent granted by Queen Elizabeth, in 1588, for trading to the river Senegal and Gambia, in Guinea; and mention is made in the archives of the neighbouring little borough of Lyme Regis of the sailing of the barque *Yonge* for Barbary.

This gentleman probably built the ancient residence before us, still known by the cognomen of "The Great House," and to him also it is probable Robert Cook, Claranceiux, in 1583, granted the coat-armour which the family afterward bore.

ARMS,—Ermine, on a bend cotized sable, three griffins heads erazed or.
CREST,—A boar's head erazed vert, armed and bristled or.
MOTTO,—"FORTITER ET PRUDENTER."

Succeeding John, came his son Walter, a stern Puritan, who was also of a literary turn, and published a little treatise entitled *A Manual, or a Justice of the Peace, his Vade Mecum,* which was deemed of sufficient importance to be enlarged and republished in 1642. He also kept a careful *Diary* during the first quarter of the seventeenth century, which has lately been discovered and published by the Camden Society.

The Yonges appear to have ever had an extraordinary penchant for Parliamentary pursuits, which followed them through their various generations, and finally culminated in their ruin.

They usually represented some of the little boroughs of their native county, and so we find of this gentleman in 1640, that a committee of the House of Commons having been appointed to ascertain what boroughs had formerly sent members to Parliament and had discontinued to do so, Honiton among others was ordered to be restored, and Walter Yonge and William Pole, Esqs., were its first representatives.

His son John was knighted by Charles I., at Ford House, Newton Abbot, Sept. 15th, 1625, and subsequently created a baronet by Charles II., 26th, Sept., 1661. He was also a sturdy politician, and was one of the hundred members secluded by Cromwell, who denied them entrance to the House, on which himself and 115 others had the courage to publish a remonstrance, asserting the legality of their right to sit there.

A curious incident is on record with regard to the state of health of this knight, and of a dispensation or license to eat flesh during Lent, afforded him by John Wilkins, the Puritan Minister of Colyton church, during the Commonwealth. It is inscribed in the register, and is as follows:—

"*Having beene certifyed by two appved physicians of ye necessity of Sir John Yongee eating flesh:—upon wch:—Having granted him a former license (so farre as in mee was)—ye same distemper agn continuing (as is certified by one of ye sd physicians) & his need of flesh being ye same,—I do as much as in mee is, give ye sd Sr. John Yonge license to eat flesh during ye sd necessity,—in witnesse wherof I have subscribed my name;—the cyth of March,* 1660.

JNO. WILKINS, Vir."

"*In ye psense of John Whicker one of ye Churchwardens.*"

The entry may possibly relate to the visitation of the Plague, as being "the same distemper again continuing."

And here we must digress for a short space to notice this old Puritan minister, John Wilkins, thus found so strangely licensing his influential parishioner to infringe on the well-known inhibition of Romish dogma. The old divine, however, appears to have had his doubts as to his qualification for such an office, and is careful twice to qualify the concession with the important proviso, "so far as in me is."

According to the characteristic words of the late Dr. Oliver, "one John Wilkins was intruded on the parishioners in 1647," and he appears to have officiated in the church till the year of the Act of Uniformity, when he resigned, and conducted his ministry in the Presbyterian Meeting-house, which has since passed into the Unitarian faith.

He died in 1667, and was buried in the vicar's vestry in the church, an erection of Canon Brerewode's, the last Romish vicar—an extraordinary pluralist, and described by the before-named learned antiquary, as having been a "very cormorant of church property."

Mutatis mutantis—the dust is the grand leveller; the grave the great husher of religious strife; not even the ingenuity of creeds can "provoke" the ear of death. Listen to the old man's epitaph: did not he know what he believed, and hath it not the conscious ring of immortality?

"Here lyes Mr. John Wilkins, minister of this place from Sep. 19, 1647, until 24 Aug., 1667.

" SVCH PILLARS LAYDE ASIDE
HOW CAN THE CHVRCH ABID
HEE LEFT HIS PVLPIT HEE
IN PATMOS GOD TO SEE
THIS SHINING LIGHT CAN HAVE
NO PLACE TO PREACH BVTS GRAVE.

LEFTS WIFE 2 SONS AND 4 DAFTERS
MARY'S LAYD HERE 8 WEEKS AFTER."

The Englishman of to-day who would sacerdotalize his religion, and entrust to his fellow man the interpretation of the charter of his spiritual freedom, as found in the majestic simplicity of his Saxon Bible, and degrade the grand old Protestant worship of his mother church into spurious sickly sentimentality and infantile ceremony, would do well to ponder over the doings of these antient fathers of our faith, rugged and stern though they be, and note well the imperishable legacy of principle they have left us.

The old Puritan Wilkins, though so "intruded," (in the estimation of his fellow-worker in the Master's vineyard), on the Colyton people, preferred in the crucial hour to renounce the privilege and emolument of being vicar of Colyton rather than subscribe to a declaration to the terms of which he conscientiously objected, still found as an attesting protest on his gravestone in the *vicar's* vestry of the church, where he had probably often in life donned his Geneva gown ere he proceeded with the ministry of the sanctuary, and which informs us, with careful truth, that he was minister of this *place*, not church, at his death.

These were times of decision and dauntless firmness; the fires of Smithfield still smouldered, and the fearless martyr spirit, the noblest achievement of human suffering, had not as yet died out in the hearts of the sons of men. Where should we find their successors now, in these days of elastic consciences and subterfuges, giving up the snug emolument even, much more pass through the fiery ordeal?

Succeeding Sir John came Sir Walter, and following him, another Sir Walter, also a great local politician, and one of the Commissioners of Customs under William III. He was a supposed adherent of the Duke of Monmouth, who during his western progress in 1680, sojourned at Great House with Sir Walter, and the room he slept in, a large bedchamber, is still known as Monmouth's room. Subsequently, in 1685, when the Duke landed at Lyme Regis, on his ill-fated enterprize, Sir Walter refused, at any rate actively, to join him—much it is said to the Duke's disappointment, who had no possible warrant to expect such a thing. However this may be, an ominous circumstance occurred afterward.

Just at this juncture Sir Walter was engaged in building a new seat at Escot, and some of the masons left the works and joined the ranks of the Duke. After the fatal fight at Sedgemoor, it is related that the brutal Jefferies ordered several of the rebels to be executed at a cross-way about a mile from Escot; a rather significant proof of this inhuman judge's suspicions. But Sir Walter survived these troubles many years, dying in 1731, leaving his title and inheritance to his son William.

We now arrive at the era of the first two statesmen, toward a notice of whom our desultory gossip has hastened us.

The former of these was the Right Honourable Sir Wm. Yonge, Bart., M.P., for Honiton, K. B., L.L.D. and F.R.S. He was created a Knight of the Bath on the re-constitution of the Order in 1755, was a Privy Councillor, and successively a Lord of the Treasury and Secretary at War.

Of Sir William's character and abilities, he is described as being the personal friend of the great statesman Sir Robert Walpole, who could speak from notes taken by him better than from any other source, and that he was a very trifling personage out of the House, but spoke as if by inspiration in it, and was gifted with a peculiar melody of voice. Lord Hervey says of him—"he had no wit in private conversation, but he was remarkably quick in taking hints to harangue upon in Parliament; he had a knack of words there that was surprising, considering how little use they were to him anywhere else. He had a great command of what is called Parliamentary language, and a talent of talking eloquently without a meaning, and expatiating agreeably upon nothing, beyond any man I believe, that ever had the gift of speech."

Notwithstanding this peculiar gift of loquacity, it should seem this garrulous placeman was very chary lest the outside world should hear what he had been saying, and consequently a great opponent to the reporters' gallery. Our modern newspaper reader will probably be surprised when he reads the following "idea" of Sir William Yonge, and then takes a glance at the report of a long debate in one of our daily papers.

On the 13th of April, 1738, Mr. Speaker Onslow, complained that there was actually "a report of their deliberations in the newspapers!"—upon which up rose Sir William Yonge, and declared his determination to have the printers punished, because said he—"they deserve to be punished, and if you do not either punish them or take some effectual method of checking them, you may soon expect to see your notes, your proceedings, and your speeches printed and hawked about the streets, while we are sitting in this House."

Poor Sir William! His busy tongue has long been silent, and as he sleeps his last long sleep in his huge leaden coffin in the corner of Colyton Church, the clang of the news-vendor's bell as it tinkles merrily in the street outside, fails now to disturb his peaceful slumber, even with visions of Parliamentary reports. He appears to have been no favourite with George II., who used to call him "stinking Yonge," and Lord Hervey (who was probably no friendly critic) further adds—"his name was proverbially used to express everything pitiful, mean, and contemptible."

But Time has long drawn its softening veil over all these political asperities, and we rather opine the race of William Yonge's, as parliamentary babblers is by no means extinct, and that the "talent of talking without meaning" is enjoyed by many an honourable senator of our present day. Sir William married Ann, daughter of Lord Effingham Howard, and died in 1755.

Thus far for the particulars relative to the history of the first of these Secretaries at War, as we have been able to gather: we now arrive at the second, in the person of the son of the preceding, known as the Right Honourable Sir George Yonge, Bart., M.P. also for Honiton, Knight of the Bath, and successively Commissioner of the Admiralty, Vice Treasurer of Ireland, Master of the Mint, and Secretary at War.

He was educated at Eton, and completed his studies at Leipzic. He endeavoured to establish the woollen manufactory at Ottery. Toward the end of his Parliamentary career he was appointed Governor of the Cape of Good Hope, where he fell under a cloud, owing to some alleged defalcations. Returning to England, he was reduced to a state of comparative indigence, and died greatly impoverished at Hampton Court, Sept. 26, 1812, aged 80. His body was brought down very privately from London, and buried at midnight in the family vault at Colyton, possibly from fear of arrest.

Thus mournfully ended the career and race of the Yonges, and of this its last representative; he had been heard to say, when possessed of nothing and in almost absolute indigence, that he commenced life with £80,000 family property, received a like sum with his wife, and the Government had paid him for his public services a similar amount. "Honiton," he exclaimed, "has swallowed all." And it is on record, upon the authority of persons but recently deceased, that on one occasion when he offered himself for re-election without the necessary qualification of money, having spent his all on them before, one of the worthy burgesses actually spat in his face in contempt. However, a complete and speedy Nemesis has recently avenged this foolish and ill-fated man's misfortunes, and Honiton has righteously disappeared from its position of undue Parliamentary importance and influence.

But a truce to these dry biographical details, which we have been quietly conning over as we have been surveying the exterior of the old mansion, and at the same time listening to the glorious tones of a thrush located somewhere within ear-shot.

"That's a beautiful bird," we remarked to a ruddy-faced brown-smocked cow-boy, who was loitering observantly near us.

"'Tis a dirsh, sur," said he, "in a cage up in the garden just round the korner, and he do keep on zinging all day most, jist like you da hear 'en now."

O delightful minstrelsy of Nature, not even confinement can check its own sweet overflow :—

> "Compared wi' these, Italian trills are tame,"—

and as we passed by after our short sojourn, the same sweet song saluted us, the remembrance of which found outlet in the following jingle some hours afterwards :—

THE COBBLER'S THRUSH.

Over the cobbler's lattice low,
  Near the village cross-ways' turn,
Where the clambering roses blow,
  And the red nasturtiums burn,—
  Whit! tu-tu-whit,—wee-ho!
There in my with-wreathed cage so white,
I sit and sing from morn to night,
And plume my speckled breast, and pry
At the passers on with my clear black eye,—
  Whit! tu-tu-whit,—wee-ho!
  Whistling loud, warbling low.

The children know me every one,
  All up and down the street,—
They love to list to my cheery tone,
  And chirrup an answer sweet;
  Whit! tu-tu-whit,—wee-ho!
The mother holds her babe aloft,
And bids him dance to my song,
And the maiden whispers a benison soft,
As she loiters her love-lorn way along,—
  Whit! tu-tu-whit,—wee-ho!
  Whistling loud, warbling low.

And the grey old cobbler hammers away
  And sings through the weary hours,—
I answer his song and whistle a lay
  From my eyrie up in the flowers;—
  Whit! tu-tu-whit,—wee-ho!
And at times he halts as the gossips bide
O'er their pitchers of water, tired,
For it fills his aged heart with pride
To hear his bird admired;—
  Whit! tu-tu-whit,—wee-ho!
  Whistling loud, warbling low.

And when his long day's work is o'er
  And shadows fall long on the lea,
The old man stands at his cottage door,
  Smokes his pipe, and talks to me,—
  Whit! tu-tu-whit,—wee-ho!
Then his white capped dame makes her garden trim,
And I wait for the dainty snail she has spied,
And when I have finished my evening hymn
They carry me safely inside.
  Whit! tu-tu-whit,—wee-ho!
  Whistling loud, warbling low.

Now let us lift the latch and explore the interior of the old domicile. An inspection within shews us the usual characteristics of a gentleman's small sixteenth century dwelling-place. Two or three parlours, passage with large winding balustrade staircase, and convenient offices behind, complete the basement; over, are numerous small bedrooms, with one chief bed-chamber, known as Monmouth's room, at the end of which, under the cornice, is a regally crowned thistle, and the cypher "J. R." beneath. A considerable quantity of old oak paneling and carving, ornament the walls.

Out of doors nothing now remains to indicate the olden gardens and pleasure grounds, except an ancient summer house. Tradition, however, tells of a spacious pleasaunce and lawns stretching away down towards the river, and that during the sojourn here of the handsome Duke, that master of dalliance with the softer sex, became enamoured of a handsome sister of his worthy host, and he used to loiter amid its flowery pastures and shady arbours, unravelling love's silken skein with the fair and accomplished daughter of the house.

Let us linger with him in fancy for awhile, and, for the nonce, idealise

A PICTURE.

She sang a quaint and antient strain,
    Within the curtained shade,
And chequered hues of varying stain,
    O'er her pale features strayed;
While from her neck a flashing chain
Reflected back the tints again,
    As there she sat and played.

'Tis o'er—those downcast eyes grow bright,
    Love-lit with archest smile,
A tapping at the window light
    Hath greeted her the while,
And chasing from her cheek the white
A mounting blush hath covered quite
    A brow that knows no guile.

She opes the casement's latch with care,
And timid bashful mien,
For well she knows who waiteth there,
As you or I, I ween;
A hand half hid in ruffles fair,
Presenting love's own emblem rare,
Reclining there was seen.

She trembles as with greeting look
She takes the proffered prize;—
Again within the curtained nook,
She sits with filling eyes;
The lute beside her lies forsook,
Her heart is now her music book,
Its sweetest music sighs.

The truant boy with mischief sure,
Hath spoilt her merry strain,
Each effort fails, love owns no cure,
All fresh attempts are vain;
Within her bosom's fastness pure,
She hides the crimson bud secure,
But cannot sing again.

Alas for Poetry and Romance—the most unimpassioned orchards, and a farmyard, now occupy the site of former attractions.

We have thus ruminated over the lives of this now well-nigh forgotten family of statesmen, and looked in at their old dismantled home. What is there further left us to find of them? Only that appointed house which all living must some day occupy—their graves.

The chancel of Colyton church consists of a central

aisle or chancel proper, and two side aisles, all of equal height and size, and is a very fine specimen of early Perpendicular work, of great regularity in design, and was probably built during the incumbency of Hugh Bridham, then vicar, at the close of the fourteenth century. After the Reformation, these side aisles or chapels were taken possession of by the two most influential families of the parish—the Poles and the Yonges—as their burial places.

In the south aisle, under the handsome array of monuments, lie the Poles; in the north, within a high, close screen of freestone, of classic design, and surmounted with the family arms and tall pinnacles, the Yonges are sepulchred. There are no monuments within whatever, but their arms and a fragment of an inscription are carved on a stone in the pavement.

A curious circumstance occurred some few years since in this mortuary enclosure. For a long period it had been used as the parish vestry, and in the centre of the room, placed there for the purpose of a table, stood the huge, antique, parish chest, A larger gathering of parishioners than usual having taken place on some special occasion, the churchwarden, a portly sized individual, standing at the head of the table, was in full harangue on the subject under discussion, when lo! all of a sudden he disappeared, amid dust and clatter, into the vault of the departed Yonges! The cave was thereupon filled up, and the writer of this, having removed the brass breastplates off the mouldering coffins, cleansed and affixed them on the adjacent walls.

We have remarked the Yonges built a new and larger residence at Escot, in Feniton parish, at the beginning of the eighteenth century. By a curious fatality this mansion was accidentally destroyed by fire about sixty years since, when everything was burnt, inclusive of family pictures and heirlooms of every description. All that now marks the former being of the house are the two old pillars of the gate-way, leading to it, in the hedgeside, near Fairmile on the road leading from Honiton to Exeter. The mansion has been since rebuilt by the Kennaway family.

We began our little history at Colyton; we shall therefore return thither to conclude it, and give the substance of a legend or two belonging to the old house, asking the reader to be a guest in imagination with us, who once, some ten years since, heard the narrative from the then living relator. We invite you to come into the large, comfortable kitchen, on a clear winter evening, and sitting yourself down on one of the two ample settles that curtain themselves out from the great blazing ingle, take note of the kind hostess, who, in company with her excellent sons, are your *vis a vis*.

There she sits erect, *petite*, neat, and with faculties clear as your own, busy with her needlecraft, with sight unaided, and yet those eyes have looked through nearly a centuries' revolving years! Listen to her story, for Mistress Mary Lane hath something to tell you of the old house she has lived so long in.

First she will inform you that she well remembers the last Secretary at War when he used to come and visit the place—a grand gentleman, of stately presence, in a rich velvet coat, wig, and ruffles, with a star on his breast, and a sword by his side, and how all the country-side stood in awe of him. Then she will tell you how late one autumn evening, when all were gone to rest, a stealthy knock came to the front door, and a strange man, dressed in deep black, bade the good master of the house arise, for the chariot of death was at the yard-gates, and a courtly victim waited its last unconscious admittance to the home of his fathers. How the parson and the grave digger were straightway summoned, and, silent and unobserved, and by the feeble glimmer of candlelight, the last possessor of the name of Yonge found holy sanctuary from the vindictiveness of man in the quiet fastness of the grave.

But this will be only half her pleasant narrative. Then she will further tell you of a circumstance that occurred many a year ago, in her younger days—how that about three o'clock one summer morning, in hay-making time, a workman arose to go to his mowing, and, going down stairs, sat himself in one of the settles, and was busily employed lacing up his boots. The grey, clear light was streaming through the old, tall, latticed casements, when suddenly he heard a sort of short clumping noise, like that made by wooden sabots, but he did not take much notice, nor raise his eyes at the instant, as he conjectured it was the dairy-maid arisen thus early, for some cause.

Opposite the settle in which sat the man is a door, opening into an inner and larger parlour, and this door was open. Inadvertently the man looked up, and was forthwith petrified with astonishment. Proceeding with short, measured, stately steps, the figure of a lady walked leisurely out of the parlour, through the corner of the room the man was sitting in, along the short passage, and up the stairs, the man hearing the receding echo of her steps as she mounted, and again all was quiet.

He minutely described her dress, which consisted of a huge farthingale of rich brocaded green silk, stomacher, and ruffles of point lace, and high-heeled shoes, and she looked neither to the right nor left. The man offered to take oath (if he did not actually do so), before a justice of the peace that lived close by, of the truth of what he saw.

No apparition has been spoken of as having been witnessed in the house since, nor is there a legend of any kind "haunting" the old fabric to account for such a sight—except one, which if true, was a very tangible and welcome appearance to the lucky beholder who, albeit, was not the poor labourer in the settle; namely, the inseperable story of a large crock of gold having been found by a former resident there, in driving through his fields one day at the rear of the house, the wheel of the cart suddenly sunk, and a large quantity of silver and gold pieces came up over the felloe.

Of course the same difficulty of believing the man's story in common with all other such narrations of the marvellous, naturally occurs; but there is something striking in this illiterate labourer being able to so well describe the details of costume he could scarcely be supposed to have ever heard of, and could not possibly have imagined so correctly.

Thus have we come to the end of our venerable hostess's story, and nearly also, to the end of our own as well. We draw a shade closer to the glowing embers, and muse awhile on what we have seen and heard. What a vast storehouse of interest is gathered in the past around us, if we would be only at the trouble of entering its portals, and exploring its mystic precincts, brimming to the full with chronicle and story. Strange mutation of human ambition, hopes, wishes, desires, that burn and glow, and sparkle, and coruscate like the crackling pile before us, and then slowly and surely subside into ashes and gloom.

Even thus, on this hearthstone of thy olden home, O spirit of the departed Yonges, we meditate, and see in the imagery of the waning fire the truthful emblem of all earthly yearnings, in their fleeting, subtle, inconstant glitter, and then silent and gradual decadence, and extinction, into darkness and oblivion; — aye

The paths of glory lead but to the grave.

But amid these chastening reflections a cheerful voice has broken their constraining spell, the ingle minstrel is shrilling out his homely song, and now another and another has joined his merry chorus, with whom we join company, and dedicate without permission our closing thoughts

TO THE CRICKET.

When mystic twilight fills the antient hall,
And on the hearth the flickering embers glow,
When fitful shadows dance on every wall,
And giant forms move round in pageant slow;—
A cheerful voice rings through the brooding gloom,
With quivering chirp, and loud increasing glee,
Soon answering echoes spring around the room,
A hidden choir of elfin minstrelsy.

Yet watch awhile—the cat, in wakeful sleep,
Sits softly purring by the glimmering fire,
See yon brown stranger from the corner creep
And in an instant to its gloom retire;—
Now a clear strain breaks from the ingle side,
And with continuous carol chants away,
Now hushed a moment—but ere echo died
Again rings forth that merry voiced lay.

Home's chorister—hid like that bird art thou
Whose far famed song is heard at evening hour,
And more are charmed to hear thy humble vow,
If it can rival not such witching power;—

The good old dame by age with silver crowned
  Protects thee ever with a favoured care,
Good luck she prophesies is always found
  Attending on thy presence everywhere.

How many breasts have throbbed around the blaze
  Unheeding thy gay song, when some fond heart
With eye abstract on the bright glow would gaze,
  Then half askant, a lurking love look dart
Tow'rds one, who in the corner half reclined,
  With much pretence, and many a vain essay
Would try thy secret hiding place to find
  When eye and thought were wandering far away,

And many a differing scene—perchance of age
  With look sedate, contented, and serene,
Hath listened to thy song, and memory's page
  Again looked o'er, and bygone days re-seen ;—
Noted alone by thy secluded eye—
  But now the drowsy clock with midnight stroke
Warns me away, and as their soft tones die,
  Thy voice alone night's solitude hath broke.

BUNKESWELL ABBEY

AND ITS

FOUNDER.

THE origin, object, and subsequent history of the old Castles and Abbeys of our land have ever proved fruitful subjects of interest and regard to antiquaries and historians, both in a general and, subordinately, in a local sense. They held conspicuous positions in the annals of civilization at the peculiar epoch in which we find their appearance—in the one case as being centres of local, social power, and in the other as seats of learning and religious feeling, doubtless exercising most important influences in the districts where they were seated, as also in the aggregate upon the nation's history. Society, then only in an incipient stage of civilized progress, was duly sensitive of the power and position conferred by the acquisition of wealth and learning; and it is easy even now, with our advanced knowledge and enlarged education, to estimate the influence they exercised, although it is probable in those days of lesser light, as compared with ours of the present, that importance was proportionately exaggerated.

Our wandering to-day is to the site (for we are told there is little else visible) of one of those antient Abbeys, founded by piously inclined hearts, in the gloom of the thirteenth century, at a lonely spot, far from the bustling haunts of men, in a green combe o'erlooking the uttermost branch of the Culm; and so we give the rein and a sympathetic cue to our thoughts, as we ascend the long hill leading toward it, anent these olden foundations and the occupation of the holy and devoted men, who lived for many an age within them and then passed away as "a tale that is told." Assuredly they had their use, and exercised their meed of good, as a very little reflection will convince us.

The humble, quiet monk, hidden within the solitude of his little cell, mainly worked away the live-long day, alternately employed in conning thoughtfully over and copying with patient industry the priceless story of Holy Writ, or well reasoned writings of the venerable fathers of the faith—or, anon, with compass and rule creating and tracing the lofty proportions and beautiful adaptations of that system of architecture whose fame is now wedded with the deathless name of his faith—or with brush and pigment slowly and cunningly elaborating those glorious illuminations that remain an equally imperishable monument of his appreciation of the beautiful in art to this day.

When he emerged from his devout and tasteful studies, he came forth to celebrate the grand and ornate worship of his Creator within the noble precincts of the adjoining sanctuary, which he had possibly designed and carefully erected to His service, amid the wondering and awe-smitten peasantry, or in privacy and loneliness to speak ghostly comfort to some sin-stricken sinner—or carry the basket of charity to the famishing cottager—or mid the ghastly horrors of the stealthy pestilence to sit by the bedside of the plague-smitten victim and direct the glazing eyes of the shriven soul to the comforts of the Cross.

Amid the dense ignorance that then existed, to deny that these men had not or did not exercise the influence for good they unquestionably possessed, and are not deserving of our present thanks and gratitude for their pious and zealous labours as custodians and transmitters of the immortal, the truthful, and the beautiful, through the long centuries of darkness and apathy in which they lived, now that their generation and office have passed away and are no more needed, would alike be disreputable to the feelings, and destructive to the finest traditions of the human heart.

Thus far, then, for the peaceful and humanizing influence of the monk, whose olden labours so many of us now-a-day are apt to challenge, and have learnt so glibly and with unappreciative indiscrimination to decry. Ignorant of his true history, some of us as a consequence, would bury him in an odium of useless idleness, bigotry, and intolerant usurpation, forgetful that when he lived the world had no other preservers of her learning, nor recognised, nor knew of a differing creed.

True, the shadows of human frailty crossed his path (as whose do they not)—a path beset with dangers and thick with difficulties, when the thirsty ambition of unchecked earthly aspirations ran like wild fire over the land. Among distracting scenes and influences the monk had only a mortal heart to rely on to guide him safely through them. Yet he often acted his important part amid the turmoil with great dignity, unselfishness and conscious integrity, that shewed he was deeply imbued with the true spirit of the religion he professed.

Therefore, let us remember him for his virtues, now that his mission has passed away, and however different and more widely expanded our present experience suggests to us the necessity of spiritual freedom and activity in our holy religion by all who profess to regard it—let us not forget there is ever this to recommend him to our gratitude, that, amid the darkest and most troublous period of our nation's history, the monk was the link that handed down to us the comprehensive principles of our common Faith, and its wondrous history, the Bible, and then in the fulness of time disappeared from our land, leaving it to gather strength, and dignity, and freedom, and repose in that Bible's light.

As we wend our way up the long hill that leads from Honiton to Dunkeswell, we do not find much in the floral world remaining to engage our attention, for the chastening presage of coming Autumn has already insensibly passed over the landscape, slightly bronzing the leaves and paling the remaining flowers. Still a few are left to attest that the engaging hand of Summer has not as yet quite lost its magic.

Here and there a stray convolvulus upturns her ephemeral silver bell, or a tall snap-dragon leans over the hedge-crest, stretching out his golden sceptre; while some members of the umbelliferous tribe occasionally congregate themselves in great force, displaying their large silvery sprent discs; and a profusion of the strong scented wild mint fills the ditches by the road side, exhibiting numerous pale purple flower dossils, on a tall bunch of which, as we slowly pass, a pair of magnificent insects, the scarlet Admiral butterfly and his wife, glance out over the hedge and settle themselves with great boldness just before us, proceeding busily to search the flowers for food.

The gloriously tinted wings of the male, as he alternately opens and shuts them to balance himself in his transit over the flower, are something wondrous to behold; his sleek jet black body and branching antennæ, his ebon and intense scarlet wings, edged with bright blue, and dotted with the purest white, are superlatively beautiful.

The handsome creature is, however, on business bent, and pays little attention to his admirers, and we silently think what kind of constituted mind it can be that would capture this lustrous insect, despoil his fairy wings of their glowing tints in the fray, and then immolate the wreck as a trophy for future admiration.

He looks a very king among others of his kind that hover near, the sober coloured delicately pencilled fritillary, and pale sheeny sulphur:—

> "The velvet nap which on his wings doth lie,
> The silken down with which his back is dight,
> His broad outstretched horns, his hayrie thies,
> His glorious colours, and his glittering eies."

But if the russet tinges of Autumn are slowly stealing the rich green out of the Summer leaves, she on her part is busily shewing the trophies of her fruity store at intervals; for anon we crook down a stray cluster (or "clapper," as it is termed in the vernacular) of well-ripened nuts, that have escaped the foraging hands and acute eyes of the school boy, or moisten our lips with a large deep purpled blackberry, for they hang in inviting profusion, or glance at the oaks studded thick with acorns—stop to admire sundry well laden apple trees in the orchards that abut the road as they droop beneath their golden and ruddy burthens, or linger at intervals to look through some gap-way and note the number of amber hued, neatly thatched stacks that cluster in the rear of the numerous farmhouses seated about the underlying valleys.

There are some good views of true Devonian landscape to be seen as we quietly mount the lengthened acclivity. After crossing the sparkling Otter, the broad fertile vale of Honiton stretches away, with the antient borough in its midst, from whose aggregation of slate roofs, shining with subdued glow in the warm sunlight, rises its high pinnacled tower, while just behind, on a knoll, the shorter substantial campanile of the old church seems to stand and keep watch over the town below.

On our right rises the ever beautiful tree-crested hill of Dumpdon, behind which is piled a massive rampart of hills, along the mid-distance of which a thin train of smoke flits along and is presently lost, while on the top a tall belvidere uprises, of strange oriental appearance, like a minaret from Jaffa or Alexandria, transplanted to one of our English hills, glancing queringly on the Christian towers underneath.

We pass Woodbine Hill, and proceeding onward loiter a few moments as we reach Wolford Lodge, to look down its luxuriantly wooded valley, and to admire some fine beeches near the lodge gates. Thence over the plateau of the hill, a good mile and a half, we turn suddenly down a lane to the left, and the village of Dunkeswell stretches itself down the little valley.

"Dunkeswell," says Polwhele, "signifies *the hill with the clear well*, and there is a remarkable well in the village called after St. Patrick, to whom the parish church is said to be dedicated, as the revel is kept on his day. This well we observe, together with numerous other clear wells or runnels of water; at one of which, that pours itself out from a spout in the hedge near the centre of the village, a lamed rustic is seated, allowing the healing freshness to trickle over the fevered limb, while two or three children are standing by, looking on with envious admiration, and evidently wishing it were their privilege instead.

We look in at the little church, which is now (as usual everywhere) being rebuilt, and are agreeably surprised to find a very fine old circular Norman font, with a roll of cable twist; above which, round the bowl, is an arcade with figures, one of which is a bishop in the attitude of benediction. There is another fine square Norman font in the adjoining parish of Luppitt.

The road leading from Dunkeswell village to the Abbey consists of a narrow veritable old English lane, some two miles in length, running along the side of the hill a considerable distance, and then it rapidly descends to a rich vale, where two or three fertile valleys meet. There we loiter awhile, detained by one of those characteristic incidents so indicative of a Devonshire lane—an almost interminable string of red dairy cows defiling slowly out of an adjoining pasture:—

MILKING TIME.

With careful step and slow,
Along the lane,
Comes with murmuring low,
The ruddy train,

Each after each, and hark!
At their rear the cow dog loud,
But his familiar bark
Frets not the docile crowd.

Eyes full as Juno's—soft,
  Lustrous and clear,—
Horns bright, and borne aloft
    O'er the lithe ear,—
Breath sweet as summer zephyr,
Perfume-laden from the flowers,—
Passes on each stately heifer
In the sunny evening hours.

On through the homestead gate
  With gentle grace,
Patiently there all await
  Each in her place;
Calmly, in blissful mood,
Ranged 'neath the shadowing trees,
Chewing contentment's cud,
Dreaming of summer leas.

Grateful their dozing glance
  Speaks a mute thanks,
As the milkmaids advance
  Steals through their ranks,—
Grudgeless flows the balmy gift,
Blessing and still blest, the while
Busy hands with movement swift
Rifle all the snowy spoil.

Having reached the bottom of the descent, we pass a cottage or two, and catch sight over the trees of the spire-shaped bell turret of the modern chapel, erected on the site of the antient Abbey church. A short turn to the left and the ruins of the Abbey gatehouse are before us.

The Abbey of Dunkeswell, a visit to the ruins of which has been the object of to-day's Wandering, received its origin from that unparalleled founder of religious establishments in Devon, William de Briwere, or Brewer, Baron of that name, in 1201.

This great nobleman, who possessed vast property and consequently exercised much influence in the county, is said to have been uncle on the mother's side to King John; and that he was an important councillor of state to that monarch and his predecessor, King Richard the First. William Brewer, who was consecrated Bishop of Exeter, in 1224, is also said to have been his grandson. To the munificence of Lord Brewer three of the numerous large religious foundations in the county owe their beginning, the Premonstratensian Abbey of Torre, the Benedictine Nunnery of Polsloe, together with this the Cistercian Abbey of the Blessed Virgin, at Dunkeswell, where he ordered his body to be buried at his decease.

Nor must it be forgotten, in describing the religious zeal of Lord Brewer, that his daughter Alice, who was wedded to Reginald de Mohun, her father's ward, founded Newenham Abbey, as we have already intimated in our Wandering to its precincts, and that her supposed effigial semblance is found in Axminster church, of which parish her father's chaplain, Gervase de Prestaller by name, was the vicar; and that the mutilated figure of the priest in the same church, lying opposite the Lady de Mohun, is considered to represent him, who, according to the Newenham chartulary, died about 1215. Besides this Lady Alice, Lord Brewer left four other daughters—Grace, Isabella, Margery and Jane, and two sons, Richard, who died during his father's lifetime, and William who survived him.

Of the history of the Abbey, during the three centuries and half of its existence little can now be recovered; but Dr. Oliver recounts a list of the sixteen Abbots that successively presided over the confraternity, the last of whom, John Ley, was apportioned a pension of £50 at the dissolution in 1540, and the Abbey itself and its estates, valued at the time in £300 per annum, was granted by King Henry VIII. to John, Lord Russell, and formed an important portion of the large ecclesiastical spoil that fell to the share of this fortunate nobleman in the county. The Abbot had, in accordance with the usual custom of monastic dignitaries, a town residence in Exeter, somewhere in St. Paul's parish. The arms of the Abbey were those of its Founder—*gules, two bends undee, or;* and the Abbey itself was dedicated to the Blessed Virgin.

Proceed we now to explore such traces of the Abbey as are left. Calling at the door of the cottage built close to the ruined gate-house, we find, as we had surmised, that the sexton and *locum tenens* of the Abbey precinct resides there, who with much willingness and considerable intelligence acts as our cicerone.

The grand entrance to the Abbey was close to the corner of the cottage, and appears to have been a broad Perpendicular arch, the gate-house with its windows and winding stone staircase was also of the same date. Inside this gateway is what is now a fine productive garden; this was probably a large outer court, originally. Through this garden you walk by a path down to the site of the antient Conventual church, on which is now built the modern chapel-of-ease. This was on the north side of the Abbey, and the shape of the church may be tolerably well traced.

Outside the wall of the church (which is now a meadow) were the Abbey buildings, stretching away in a straight line southward, some two hundred feet or nearly, forming apparently one side of a square that size, that embodied probably the Abbey precinct, at the extreme edges of which occur a few pieces of broken wall. The chatty sexton informs us that during the dry summer months the plan of the Abbey buildings in the meadow are easily traceable, from the grass withering over the old foundations. He says that, apparently, a long passage stretched away from the transept of the church, with chambers at each side, other divisions occurred inside, and at the end of this long series of chambers was one very large one.

In digging graves near the new church (the present yard being the site of the previous church belonging to the Abbey), a number of skeletons have been found of the religious formerly residing here, the antient mode of sepulture being very apparent, the bodies being buried without coffins, and a row of stones set roof-shaped along, just above, to prevent the earth falling immediately on them. A quantity of encaustic tiles and portions of pillars and carved stone-work have been dug up. A lot of these antient tiles are reset in the pavement of the new church—on some of them is a shield *checquy*, others display *an elephant towered*, and a *lion rampant between crosslets.*

In the corner of the present enclosed churchyard is a large stone coffin, one of two, discovered in a singular way. We have remarked that in the meadow adjoining, during dry weather, the traces of the foundations of the old conventual buildings are clearly traceable. At the further extremity of them, in the apparently large room at the end, a small square spot a short distance off the wall, was observed to give up and get dry much quicker than any of the rest, and became quite noticeable.

Suspecting something peculiar was beneath, the ground was opened, and at about a foot below the surface two large stone coffins side by side were discovered. These coffins were six feet six inches long, and of the usual shape, with a circular opening for the head, and a smaller furrow at the base to receive the heels. The covers were of Purbeck marble, and had been polished, but there was no ornament except the antient cavetto moulding round the edge. On raising the lids, two very perfect skeletons were seen, not a bone displaced; and they were pronounced by a neighbouring surgeon to be male and female. The bones were carefully gathered into the most ruinous of the two coffins, and buried within the Abbey church; the other coffin being left above ground for the inspection of the wandering antiquary.

Who were the tenants of these old sarcophagi, and how came they buried so far from the Conventual church? We think there is little doubt that these coffins contained the remains of the Founder, Lord Brewer, and his lady, and that this large inclosed site where they were discovered, was the more ancient chapel of the Abbey, in use before the larger conventual church was finished; that their burial place was probably never afterwards disturbed, but the chapel was set aside as a mortuary one, where a daily mass was said for the repose of their souls. An ancient chapel similar to this presumed one holds a relative situation to the Abbey buildings in the adjoining foundation of Newenham.

As we looked into the gloomy receptacle and thought of the former glories that once upreared themselves around, our imagination sought to depict the noble pair—he the uncle and councillor of Kings, in his close-fitting hauberk and coif of sparkling ring mail, silk enfolded surcoat of cunning embroidery, with his huge sword, and kite-shaped shield, bearing the broad, wavy golden bands of Brewer stretched athwart a vermillion field, on his arm — she, in snowy wimple and robes of costly stuff by her lord's side.

But these courtly splendours are all gone—the emblazoned noble and richly draped ecclesiastic have long been hidden in the shadowy region of the past, and their semblance only exists in the eye of fancy. The lark and the linnet now chant the orisons and vespers that have long ceased, and been silent in this their ancient wonted abode—the bee and the butterfly are the only pilgrims that visit and linger around these deserted shrines—and the dew-laden daisy the only mourner that droops and weeps over these unmarked sepulchres, when

> "At night the pale moon cometh
> And looketh down alone."

Of the external form of the structure no record or tradition exists—but the style of architecture of the church may be safely assigned to the Early English or lancet period (being attested by some capitals of columns, and fragments of polished marble shafts continually discovered in the soil beneath) and its dimensions were evidently of considerable size, as were also the conventual buildings attached.

These few crumbling foundations, then, are all the scant evidences left to attest the former being of the spacious buildings that once upreared themselves on the greensward before us, to conceive the semblance of which is now left to the subtle and ingenious creation of fancy. "Its ruins lie low on the ground," wrote Risdon two centuries ago. No truer description can be given now; and again we are standing on one of those hallowed spots, whose holy precincts so often consecrate the green valleys and plains of our land, and are invested with imperishable associations, though scarcely one stone is left upon another to point out their locality.

Like its ruined sister foundation, Newenham, the kindly flower-bespangled lap of Nature treasures within its gracious sanctuary hundreds of quiet, pulseless forms, now hushed in the arms of death within these hidden chambers of the grave—even the Founder, the sixteen Abbots, and all the religious confraternity through the three centuries of their abode in this sylvan solitude.

RESURGAM.

Creator of our spirits, bright—
Our eyes search through this life's short night
For closer glimpses of Thy light.

Thy quickening light—whose glances play
Irradiant o'er thoughts subtle way,
Or blossom paints with viewless ray.

And if Thyself we may not see,
Yet Thine is ours perpetually,
Where eye may roam or thought may flee.

The germ immortal Thy love did
First in the soul cause to be hid,
Doth for fruition ever bid.

Time's trackway, dim to mortal eye,
Seems but to lead where all must die,
Yet 'neath Thy glance no death is nigh.

Our cold-soled feet rest on this clay,
Our eager glances bend away,
Toward the realm of endless day.

Not ever thus our sight will be,
But merged and mingled soon shall see
The finite in infinity—

Through that dark arch all edged with fire;
Where human yearnings swift expire,
Lost in the thoughts for Thee that tire.

When eyelids close from this world's pride,
One short sharp mortal pang—then wide
The doors of glory swift divide.

Then for the spirit's ærial form
And blazing wings to flee the storm
Where sins allure and doubts deform;—

And reach the rest, contented, pure,
Filled with the peace that must endure
In Thee full satisfied, secure.

Having surveyed to the full, and with as much precision as may be, the few ruinous fragments that are now left to attest the size and importance of the olden Abbey of Dunkeswell, our steps lead us out into the underlying plot of rich pasture on the north side, still called "Churchyard Meadow" (having been perhaps originally the ordinary burial ground of the community), and mounting on a friendly stile, beside which babbles along the invariable attendant on a monastic institution, a bright clear rill, one of the outermost progenitors of the Culm, we give ourselves up for a few minutes to contemplation and rest.

The new district Church and neat School-house are before us, raised there to perpetuate the memory and purpose of the dismantled foundation. But where is that olden stately Church with its heaven directed pinnacles, and the ample pile of buildings that adjoined it? Gone—all gone, the temple and its priests, the house and its occupiers—even the very coffin of its founder lies untenanted and uncared for; while the wondering rustic of to-day looks into its massive depths with vague curiosity, and scans the huge adamantine foundations around as the traces of some former mystic age, whose history and use are alike to him incomprehensible, so completely have humanising merciful laws—a differing education, however imperfect, and the wondrous liberty of an open Bible everywhere, left these antient appliances of religion in oblivion.

The dust of the old fraternity slumbers beneath the green-sward—there undisturbed it has remained for nigh three hundred years, desolate and unregarded—

now, another temple, dedicated to the same Great Being, but with a simpler and purer faith, has again arisen on the old foundation, through the munificence of pious hearts, perpetuating the holy mission of its predecessor; and though no gorgeous robed ecclesiastics sweep through the polished aisles, nor keep solemn vigil at shrine and tomb, yet the clear views of unfettered truth are constantly proclaimed within its antient precincts, unaided by useless ceremonial, to win their sure majestic entrance into the human soul. Once more, too, when this mortal coil is shuffled off, the dust of the present generation is brought to mingle with that of the monks of old.

But we must bring our reverie to a close, for the deepening gloom of evening has stolen an imperceptible march upon us, and to our fancy's eye the turreted gable, roof-line and adjoining trees have assumed the proportions of a great conventual Church, and the old hoary gnarled gate post in the hedge below, with its encircling chain and padlock, seems to gaze at us through the shadows with the semblance of some grey cloaked and cowled Cistercian friar, with his rosary at his girdle.

So we move off from our resting place, and rapidly thread our way up the long steep lane leading back to Dunkeswell. The tall hedges and overhanging trees make our path more than usually gloomy, but afford as a recompense a good view of the spangled canopy above, wherein the stars are shining with a strange brilliancy for the time of the year, but which may be accounted for somewhat, as the temperature is grown quite chilly.

We have a "good step" yet ere the autient borough be reached, but the clime and the hour are alike most pleasant. We pass a cottager's wife or two hurrying homeward from the town with basket of errands, but otherwise find no company, save the occasional hum of a beetle driving heedlessly by, once or twice in unpleasant proximity to our auditory organs.

Thou hast wings, too, thou ebon mailed elf of the twilight, we cogitate, as we remember the beautiful apparition of the morning's butterfly, and "improve the occasion and circumstances" mentally as we pursue our solitary walk down over the hill. Here is the result:—

THE BUTTERFLY AND THE BEETLE.

O slender form, and wings of diaper,
Banded with tessera of richest tint,
Whose deep soft glow, shewn in the sunshine clear,
Would almost shame the flashing gems' fierce glint—
Why are thy wings so lustrous and so large,
With beauty all besprent from marge to marge?

Why hast thou thus a form of life and joy,
Careering ever—clad in angel guise—
Sipping ambrosia with untiring cloy,
As if earth's common lot thou didst despise;
And had no resting for thy dainty feet
Save on those odorous petals blooming sweet.

The armoured beetle, clad with darkening sheen,
Creeps slowly on his earth-road all the day,
Nor cares to mount the luscious flower between
The barren stages of his dreary way;
Wings hath he too, as thee, but the bright day
Ne'er tempts him to upmount and soar away.

Yet when the shadows of the evening come,
And clustering dewdrops weep from leaf and spray,
He speeds him upward from his weed-built home,
Winging his heedless and uncertain way
Through miry glade, o'er fen and rush-grown waste,
Then, in the gloom, unnoticed drops in haste.

There is an earth and heaven, ye say to me,
One tearful, dark,—the other sunny, bright;
Creatures ye are of both—and this to thee
Unseals our pictured lessons to thy sight;
To day (thy night) the beetle's path ye wend,
To morrow, with a seraph's wings ascend.

COLCOMBE

AND THE

DEVONSHIRE ANTIQUARY.

"OF what use is the study of antiquities," saith one—"pouring over a musty manuscript, inspecting a crumbling ruin, tracing the history of those long since returned to their parent dust, rubbing an old coin, deciphering an antient deed, and such like?"

The Present, argue these utilitarian mentors, is the sphere for active thought and speculation—to seize the passing moment as it speeds on its fleeting way, make the best of *it*, and if you can, covet and pursue that rarer wisdom which lays hold of and draws from it a presage of future prospects, ever ready to be turned to your advantage and happiness;—but as for the Past, there is little to be remembered with pleasure—the shadows of failure in that picture ever overpowered the brighter lights of success—therefore let the dead bury their dead.

So in general urges the thoughtless, restless, world —the certainty of a Past, some day surely swallowing our little life as a small paragraph in a page of its Lethean history, causes a revulsive chill to creep over our feelings, as we accept without demur the seemingly far off but certain dèstiny—that in a few short years, a half century at farthest, no living representative of our acquaintanceship or kinship will be left, who had seen or known, or valued, or loved us—and that the time is fast hastening when the last living link of our chain of acquaintanceship will be snapped by the hand of death, and then our short undistinguished lives will subside unnoticed as a little passing wave in the great ocean of eternity. No one will seek to inquire further of us, or about us: the voice of Memory falters as she pronounces "dust to dust," while Time at her side inscribes the word *Fuimus* on our sepulchre.

It is one of the grateful provinces of the Antiquary, and not the least attractive, to fill in some measure this apparently, cheerless, hopeless, aching void. With a scrupulous, reverend, unbiassed affection, he examines the Past, its people and their works, and seeks with zealous, close-bent attention, if not affection, to give its seemingly "airy nothings" a "local habitation and a name,"—reclothe their inanimate forms with garb of words, embalm their histories in the imperishable cerements of literature, and thus recall and re-display glimpses of that wondrous, vast, invisible world, whose margin is for ever stealthily and silently enlarging.

But the charm of this exploration can only be felt

in its fulness by those who lovingly and carefully pursue it. And the interest awakened is ever indefinable and unsatisfied. As with a magician's wand the Antiquary raises the shadowy curtain, and scene after scene, and character after character, passes in endless review—and a mighty world invisible to the ordinary eye, of unceasing activity and importance, continually reveals and expands itself.

Thus, to such an enquirer the resources and advantages of two worlds are ever open, of which the Present as compared with the Past is but a cipher. It may be said, perhaps with some semblance of truth, that his explorations are cold and passionless, as being devoid of tho charm of living reality, and shorn alike of the warmth and loveable interest of to-day's incidents. But to this it may be answered, that he addresses himself to these unravelments of old histories and investigations of persons and things, with the unprejudiced and therefore ever beautiful and enduring attributes of truth — with no covert desire to serve or damage the subject under review—and though the glittering wings of Romance aro forbidden him, as they justly should be, yet as human life is ever fuller of the wonderful than Fancy's most exuberant creations, so the episodes of former existences are fraught to the full with forgotten scenes of interest and wonder, quite as startling and uncommon as those occurring in tho present hour, and in no-wise needing the unreal tinsel of fictitious exaggeration to commend themselves to our notice and interest.

To trace, elucidate, preserve, chronicle and put on record all that has been thus interesting, as comprised within the work or sequence of human hearts, minds, or hands, is the peculiar province of the Antiquary—to walk round the crumbling citadel of Memory and point her walls with the ever-during cement of human interest—examine and keep sound the shadowy chain of Time, burnish and weld its change-frayed, rust-eaten links—connect with quiet loving industry the continuous cycle of Existence and preserve it ever fresh and green.

It is with thoughts such as these that we step out of the railway carriage at the Shute Junction of the little branch railway to Seaton, and set out on our walk down the meadows to Colcombe, the residence of Sir Wm. Pole, the industrious Devonshire antiquary. It is a broiling hot day in early July, and the beautiful pyramidal hill of Shute Park appears on our right, garnished with magnificent trees; and between us and it a subtle mirage is playing over the hot, dry, iron road, that seems to lead up like a path to its

> Breezy steeps—
> Cool glades, and shades umbrageous.

Before us, some mile and half down the panting valley, lies the little town of Colyton, nestling amid the elms, while further on beyond we catch the clear, blue line of the eternal sea.

Out over the hedge;—ah! 'tis hay-making time—how delightful the balmy fragrance! A plague on these "labour-saving" machines of our Yankee cousins, they invade everything—from old Aunt Grace's work-box and needle-craft—good, wholesome, home-sewn shirts and their slop rivals—to the poetry of the hay-field. This incessant burr of the turner and clank of the horse-rake is but a sorry apology for the old-fashioned rows of jovial hay-makers and their inevitable fun; neither is the hay so made much more than half as good. And these mowing machines, too, have put the musical whet of the scythe to flight in many a place;—our Devonshire valleys, however, with their undulations and watering channels, are rather queer patients for the machinery doctors, and the machines often leave as much as they cut.

Through an open gateway, and our self-made path takes us along the course of the little Umborne brook, that is hurrying away down the valley to meet her elder half-sister, the Coly; and the inviting shadow of a large elm prompts us to sit down a few minutes on the grass, and rest awhile, to enjoy the beauty of the season and scene.

The little river is babbling away at our feet, and up its clear shining current a snowy white duck and her tribe of brown ducklings are busily working their way—now diving in the shallows for some luckless worm, now threading with great celerity the mazes of a thicket of reeds and fleur-de-lys, whose tall, spear-shaped leaves and golden flower finials tremble, as the busy brood bustle in and around. At a short distance below, a large mass of alder grows out from the hedge, o'er-arching the river in grateful shade, and here, knee-deep in the water, five or six sleek Devons, with their noses thrust in under the boughs, have taken refuge from the heat and from worrying flies, which, nevertheless, are still contriving to keep up the assault, as the impetuous glint of the white horns, and swirl of the angry tail, sending a shower of spray around, give us due notice of at intervals—and now, tired of the incessant infliction, they are off, tail on end, in mad gallop, round the meadow, now back again, snorting and staring, to their place of refuge.

But the passing rush of a railway train warns us that time is fleeting, and walking along the skirt of a fine upland meadow, called the Lawn, we soon find ourselves standing before the picturesque ruin of Colcombe, whose last inhabitant was the celebrated Devonshire antiquary, Sir Wm. Pole.

The first resident at Colcombe, and who built the original house there, was Hugh Courtenay, Baron of Okehampton, who flourished about the middle of the thirteenth century. He is noted for having had a great quarrel with the Abbot and Monks of the neighbouring Abbey of Ford, of which monastery he was patron, relative to certain services they refused to render him.

This nobleman's father, Lord John, had been "unco guid" to the holy fraternity there; but his son, Hugh, was not so liberally inclined, and claimed his due; at which the monks rebelled, and refused to accord him, whereupon the irate Peer, taking the law into his own hands, with a large company of retainers, made a sudden raid upon the pastures of the Abbot, and drove away all his cattle. The beasts were duly re-plevined, and a great lawsuit raged awhile. Peace, however, such as it was, came at last, but Lord Hugh had not swallowed his revenge, and accordingly, says Cleveland, "on Sunday after the feast of St. Agatha, the Virgin, A.D. 1290, as he was returning to his house, at Colcombe, through the Grange of Westford, he again took away a bull and twelve cows, four oxen and four heifers,—and so he revived the lawsuit that had been made up between him and the Abbot Nicholas, which would have been at great charge and damage to Lord Courtenay, if the Abbot had not, out of respect to his patron, withdrawn his suit.

But the Lord Hugh Courtenay, being thus provoked, had the Abbey of Ford always in hatred, and never did the monks any kindness afterward. He added Whitford and Colliton to the inheritance of his ancestors, the moiety of which he had from his uncle, William de Courtenay, who had them with his lady, a daughter of Thomas Bassett, and the other moiety he purchased himself, and he built a house at Colcomb, in Colliton parish, and died there, February

28th, 1291, and was buried at Cowick, near Exon."

His wife was Eleanor, daughter of Hugh de Spencer the elder, Earl of Winchester, one of the unfortunate favourites of the equally unfortunate Edward II. "She lived a widow above thirty years, and governed her house at Colcombe with great prudence, for she was a lady that did excel in wisdom, and much given to hospitality." She followed her lord to his grave at Cowick, October 1st, 1328.

People of strong powers of will were these founders of Colcombe, altogether a remarkable pair, of decidedly English proclivities.

Succeeding this noble couple, their son Hugh was doubtless domiciled at Colcombe—and there is complete evidence that their grandson Hugh, a celebrated representative of this antient family, who married Margaret, daughter of Humphry de Bohun, Earl of Hereford and Essex, Lord High Constable, by his wife Elizabeth, daughter of Edward I., lived there.

There is in the possession of the Chamber of Feoffees, of Colyton, a deed-poll, relative to a conveyance of a burgage at Colyford from "*Hugo de Courtenay, junior,*" to "*Johanni Wylemot de Culiford et Juliana uxoris ejus,*" dated "*apud Colcombe,*" in the year 1340. Attached to the deed is his heraldic seal, which contains the arms of Courtenay, with a label of three, while over the shield is the golden mullet of his mother, who was Agnes, the sister of Lord St.

John of Basing, and a portion of the border inscription also remains.

They had a fruitful progeny of seventeen children, and their bones are sepulchred under the second arch from the choir of the south aisle, in the nave of Exeter Cathedral; but their recumbent effigies have been removed to the south tower, *renovated* in all the suppositious glory of nineteenth century stucco.

No further evidence reaches us of the sojourn of this noble family here, till we arrive at the era of that beautiful little enigmatical monument in Colyton Church, where a girlish form, with coronet on her head, and an array of regally quartered escutcheons over, speaks of her illustrious lineage.

Tradition tells of her as having been Margaret, daughter of Earl William and Katharine his wife, seventh daughter of Edward IV., choked by a fish bone, at Colcombe, A.D. 1511; but she is known to have been living many years afterwards, and the correct history of this sepulchral figure will probably ever remain a mystery.

Within a fretted niche, a child-like form
Reclines with hands uplifted as in prayer,
A hundred years thrice told Time's surging storm
Hath passed, and still left thy memorial here;
Angels are watching o'er thee with fond care,
In semblance sweet thy tomb to guard and grace;
A coronet is on thy brow,—but there
A bright unfading crown hath long had place,
Which no rude earthly hand may mar, nor yet efface.

The little children come and gaze on thee
With half averted face, then turn away
With fearful furtive glance; hushed is their glee
As through the grassy churchyard slow they stray,
Timid their steps, recounting on their way
With infant voices weak, how thou didst die,
Young as themselves, as artless and as gay;—
The sad tale over, homeward all they hie,
Each with a sorrowing heart, each with a tearful eye.

On the attainder of the unfortunate Henry Courtenay, Marquis of Exeter, by his uncle, Henry VIII., that vindictive king disposed of a large portion of the Colyton property; but Queen Mary restored to the Earl Edward Courtenay, all such lands as had not been alienated. Dying without issue, the manor reverted to the four sisters of Earl Edward, so created by King Henry VII.; and one moiety of the Colyton property, that descending by Maud, wife of John Arundel, of Talvern, containing Colcombe Castle, was purchased by William Pole, Esq., of Shute, who settled it on his son, Sir William, and he subsequently purchased the other sister's interest.

"A goodly bwilding," saith the Antiquary, "was here intended by the last Erles, but altogether unfinished; and nowe the whole beinge reduced from all ye coheires into my possession, I have newe built the howse and made it the place of my residinge."

Thus have we brought the history of the venerable ruin before us down to the period when we find the zealous and learned Antiquary at home in his house here. In every way suitable to his tone of mind, and congenial to his antiquarian taste, must the associations connected with the place have been; nor could an apter site have been offered for his domicile than this old foundation of the Courtenays, the most celebrated family of our shire, and to use the words of Mr. Davidson, "the stamp of whose almost princely authority may be extensively recognised throughout the county."

Here, then, is Colcombe; and these massive ruins before us are all that remain of the "howse" the Antiquary "newer built."

The mansion appears to have been somewhat considerable in size, and of oblong shape—one end, apparently the kitchen, is still roofed over, and contains a chimney of enormous dimensions, and a high wall—covered with luxuriant ivy at one end, and exhibiting along its face Tudor windows and doorways—rears itself in massive outline over the spectator. Within all is ruinous and dismantled.

During the residence of the Courtenays, there was a domiciliary chantry attached to the house—traces of its ruins are to be seen at the back, and it was endowed with some lands near the still clinging cognomen of "Chantry Bridge" in the meadows below, which were sold to the Erle family at the dissolution.

A curious arrangement will arrest the notice of the visitor in the little stream or river that runs *under* the house. This brook is a kind of leat or canal, brought artificially, evidently, from the Umborne, about a mile above, along the side of the hill to Colcombe, where it passes under the house, and, flowing on, turns Colcombe mills, a quarter of a mile below. It is probable that Colcombe, as it now stands, was not the original position of the ancient house,—foundations, of a circular tower-shaped form, are found in a field near the entrance gateway, below the stream, and it is possible the water was conveyed thus for filling the old castle moat, irrigating the grange meadows, and driving the manorial mill.

As the Antiquary rebuilt the house, how came it to be so soon a mass of ruins? Thereby hangs a tale, full of strange presumptions, perhaps of revenge of some sort.

"Walter Erle, which had been servant unto Kinge Edw. 6, Queene Marye, and Queene Elizabeth," says the Antiquary, purchased at the dissolution the manor of Axmouth, and also the chantry lands at Colcombe. This is unquestionably the Walter Erle mentioned in the Colyton church register as "being of Colcombe, gentleman, and who was wedded to Marye Weeke," daughter and heir of Roger Weeke, of Bindon, Axmouth, in 1549, and three of their children are noticed as being baptized from Colcombe. This gentleman, without doubt, was resident there.

Thomas Erle, described as "of Charborough" on the monument of the Antiquary's father, in Colyton church, married Dorothy Pole, the sister of the Antiquary. In his account of Bindon, Sir W. Pole speaks of his nephew, Sir Walter Erle, as living there in "his house with fayre demesnes thereunto belonging." He mentions him as being the son of Dorothy, the daughter of William Pole, of Shute, Esq., but does not say who his brother-in-law was.

There can be no doubt but this was the Thomas Erle, then of Charborough, and son of Walter Erle and Mary Weeke, of Colcombe; for in another place it is mentioned that Sir Walter Erle, of Axmouth, was the son of Thomas Erle.

This Sir Walter Erle, who was occasionally M.P. for Lyme Regis, was knighted by James I. in 1616. In 1627, the sturdy knight resisted one of those forced loans which the unfortunate Charles I. exacted from his unwilling subjects, and was forthwith committed to the tender mercies of the Fleet prison, and the day of hearing put off; but being subsequently brought up upon a writ of *habeas corpus* in the King's Bench, as a matter of course, "upon solemn argument it was found for the king against him," and he was thereupon re-committed to jail, where he remained about twelve months.

Sir Walter did not forget this indignity when the proper time for retaliation presented itself, as we shall see. The troubles of Charles soon increased, and in 1642, Sir Walter, then resident at Axmouth, seized Lyme Regis, and garrisoned it for the Parliament, on which side he was well fortified from his supposed marriage with a daughter of Sir William Waller, the Parliamentarian General; although he subsequently allied himself with the heiress of Dymock, of Warwick, as appears from the monument in Axmouth church.

Sir William Pole, the Antiquary, had now been dead seven years, and his grandson, Sir William Pole, knight, resided at Colcombe. The Poles were Royalists, the Erles, Parliamentarians.

Prince Maurice, marching westward in aid of the king, came from Beaminster to Colyton, fixing his quarters at Colcombe Castle. From this he made an attack on Stedcombe House, the newly-erected residence of Sir Walter Erle, which was garrisoned by him for the Parliament, and, after a strong fight, captured the house and burnt it down. Afterwards, on the 25th July, 1644, in company with Lord Henry Percy, they alarmed the garrison at Lyme, and then retired back to their quarters, Percy's regiment returning to Colyton.

"The insulted garrison," says Mr. Davidson, "determined to requite the visit, and lost no time in despatching on the same night a party of 120 horse, commanded by Captains Pyne, Bragge, and Erle, who surprised the Royalists so effectually, that a major and other officers, 55 men, 100 stand of arms, 120 horses, and good pillage, fell into their hands, and the regiment was entirely dispersed." This was no doubt the date when the lordly domicile of Colcombe was destroyed. They had burnt Erle's house at Axmouth, and now Colcombe shared the same fate, Captain Erle joining in the fray. Some years ago a rusty cannon ball was found in the ruins.

Merciless exactions followed on the Royalists, and Sir William Pole was amerced to the Parliament as a delinquent in the sum of £2,855. Subsequently, when the Restoration came about, we find him petitioning for an indemnity of his losses occasioned by the garrison of Lyme having plundered his houses at Colyton and Colcombe. The damages were estimated at £10,000, the loss at Colcombe alone including half that sum! As the chances of re-imbursement were small, it is inferred that the estimates were increased in like proportion; but history is silent as to what he got repaid to him.

Thus the glory departed from Colcombe, and the story has a strange appearance. Two cousins, ranged on differing sides of political controversy of the deadliest import, lived in stately mansions in a valley within sight of each other. From the one an armed force sallied forth and razed the fair proportions of the other to the ground; in a few days its compeer shared a similar fate at the hands, most probably, of its opponent. How many fine old country seats succumbed to the devastating hand of war at this troublous period of our nation's history, while those fierce struggles for political and religious power urged men's passions on to relentless animosity, though often previously tied to each other in social friendship, or as in this case, by near relationship—changed by conflicting ideas of liberty into the sternest enmity and distrust.

Stedcombe was subsequently rebuilt by the Halletts, who purchased it of the Erles; but Colcombe still lies in ruins.

List, stranger, list, and do not harshly tread
Within these roofless and deserted halls,
Thy footsteps mock the sounds which long have fled
And echo strangely 'mid these crumbling walls.
Each noise that stirs, a past event recalls,
And wakens to new life some long lost scene,
Which grows illusive on the sense, and falls
With deepest impress on the mind serene,
Lit to refulgence with a rich ideal sheen!

For 'tis a haunted place,—heard ye not clear
The rustling sweep of female tread so light,
Flitting like airy spirit on your ear
With tripping glee as if fraught with delight?
Methinks from yonder paneless casement's height
I see the light wind carelessly unbind
The glossy curling tresses, clustering bright
Around some fair girl's face; but oh! I find
'Tis Fancy's subtle gleams upon my teeming mind.

A firmer step—Through the long passage dank
The hollow echoings seem louder grown,
Reverberating wildly, till they sank
Soft as the flowing riv'lets gurgling tone:—
There in yon doorless aperture of stone
He seems to stand, in state firm and erect:
But Time his mansion in decay hath strown,
And left us nought but grey walls to inspect,
As silent vestiges to muse o'er and reflect.

But now the setting sunbeam brightly gilds
Each broken battlement and mouldering tower,
While in each crannied nook the spider builds,
His fortalice, to every drooping flower ;—
And fairies hold their court in witching hour,
And fealty dance around the moss-clad stones,
Beneath the canopy of floral bower
Led by the grasshopper's quick blithesome tones,
When midnight solitude the still air closely zones.

Here where was resonant both joke and smile,
Where beauty mingled oft with worth and grace,
And jocund mirth did weary hours beguile,—
The bat alone now finds a dwelling-place ;
Nought but the ivy's cherishing embrace,
And weeds with wavy tuft, and lichens green,
Now linger near these walls, where many a race
Of chieftains high and lordly once were seen ;
The only monuments that such as these have been.

Yet strong e'en in decay, these ruins still
Shall firmly stand, and Time's sure hand defy,
While at its base the swiftly flowing rill,
Shall, as of old, still gently murmur by ;—
And many a summer's breeze shall round it sigh,
And many a rude and blighting winter blast ;
And generations oft shall rise and die ;
But it so void and waste, shall yet hold fast,
And to succeeding years with dim renown still last.

Of the distinguished individual, the ruins of whose residence we have been exploring, or of his merits as the correct and indefatigable Antiquary of our county, it is only a work of supererogation to speak in praise. To his large and careful *Collections* every succeeding man employed in investigating any portion of the history of Devon has to make continual application for information—the which, but for its having been safely chronicled there, would, for many years gone by, have sunk beneath the reach of memory. It is not intended to enter here into any extended biographical notice of his life, an excellent memoir of which may be found in the ever useful Prince. According to the Colyton Register,

"*William Pole sonne of William Pole was chrystened the xxvii daye of Auguste,*—1561."

He was the son of the said Wm. Pole, Esq., of Shute, by his wife Katherine, daughter of Alexander Popham, of Huntworth, in the county of Somerset, Esq. The family of Pole is of very ancient and distinguished descent, the Antiquary being the seventh in direct succession of the Devonshire branch. He studied first at Exeter College—choosing the profession of the law, entered the Inner Temple, and being called to the bar, was elected successively Autumn Reader, Double Reader, and finally Treasurer. Returning to Devonshire, he was Sheriff of the County for the years 1602-3—but a sad trial awaited him in 1605, when he lost his wife through an accident. She is buried in Colyton Church, where is her statue, kneeling, habited in a black gown, ruff and cap, with her four sons kneeling in front, and her five daughters behind. Below is this inscription :—

"Heere lyeth ye body of Mary late wyef of Sr. Wm. Pole of Shute knig: beinge ye eldest daughter and on of ye foure heires of Sr. Wm. Periham of Folford Kng: Lo: Chief Baron of ye Kinge Maiesties Excheqver shee left behind her 4 sones and five davghters vnto her saide husband viz.—John, Periham, Will:, and Frauncis, sones,—and Mary, Katherine, Elizabeth, Ann, and Elioner, daughters —shee brought vnto him also 2 other sones, viz. Wil: her firste child and Arthure beinge one of ye 3 sones wich she brought at one birth, and perished by an vnfortvnate fall, she dyed ye 2nd of May in ye yeare of our Lord, 1605, being then of the age of 38 and on month, and married vnto her hvsband 22 years and tenn months."

A young wife when married, only fifteen years old —and a melancholy fate for so fruitful a mother, still in the prime of life. In the year following his wife's death, the Antiquary received the honour of knighthood from the hand of King James I., at Whitehall, on the 5th February, 1606.

It is probable Sir W. Pole pursued with unremitting industry his favorite investigation during the larger portion of life, for forty or fifty years at least; for it appears he was busily transcribing and collecting in 1599. The result of this labour shewed itself at his death in the completion of several "vast manuscript volumes in folio, big as Church bibles,"—some portions of which were unfortunately lost during the troublous period of the Civil Wars. A valuable selection from the above recited abundant storehouse was printed by his descendant, Sir J. W. de la Pole, Bart., in 1791, and we believe the original MS. is now deposited in the British Museum.

Of his numerous issue, the worthy Antiquary lived to see many of them allied to representatives of some of our most honoured county families. His eldest surviving son, John, was also knighted, and afterwards, during his father's lifetime, created a baronet by King Charles I., on 12th September, 1628.

Calmly and industriously pursuing his favourite investigations, amid the eventful times that overhung his native land, it is probable that he peacefully passed the latter years of his life.

"He was," says Prince, "endowed with excellent parts, and adorned with great accomplishments; and, as what enamels and adds loveliness to all the other, beautified with a very civil, courteous and obliging carriage and disposition, which indeed is the true gentility. He was learned also; not only in the laws, but in other polite matters; he was very laborious in the study of antiquities—especially those of his own county—and a great lover of that venerable employment; insomuch he thereby became as the first and best antiquary (for certainty and judgment) that we ever had; it being plain that with this gentleman's labours, most of those who wrote since on this argument have adorned their works. But at length death (that *ultima Linea rerum*) came and added a period to the last line of his life; though not until he had lived to a very great age. He lies interred in the parish Church of Colliton, under a flat stone, whose inscription is obliterated by time."

There is an original picture of the antiquary in Shute House: the countenance has a grave, thoughtful expression, and the whole portrait a striking Cromwellian contour and massiveness. The date of his burial is thus described in the Colyton Register:—

"*Sir William Pole, Knight, was buried the X daye of Marche*, 1635."

but according to a certificate from the College of Arms, appended to his published *Collections* he is said to have died on the 9th of February preceding, at his house of Colcombe, in the 74th year of his age.

From the appearance of the pavement in the Pole aisle of the Church there does not appear to have been any memorial, either by flat stone or otherwise, to this celebrated man, but we believe it is intended, by his descendant, the present respected Baronet, to supply this deficiency at an early date.

Having looked well over the ruins and explored the dark recess of the building in the rear, which was apparently the ancient chapel, now tenanted by the inevitable cider hogsheads, we direct our steps into the orchard adjoining, and here the terraces and slopes are plainly traceable of the olden pleasaunce garden, on one of the little grassy plateaus of which an immense number of sweet scented jonquils are in full blow, and are doubtless a relic of its former attractions, embalmed by the kindly hand of Nature.

From this we enter a fine upland meadow called "Wellclose," so termed from an ancient well found in its centre, and intended probably to supply the mansion with pure water. The well itself consists of an arched recess in the side of the hill, about two hundred yards from the house; in front is an elliptic arch, containing foliage and shields in the spandrils, with iron hooks by the side, where originally a door was placed. A fine spring of water rises inside, and flows down a channel in the meadow to the house below. Over the well rise a number of wild cherry trees, which form with the old archway a very picturesque object during blossom-time; and the view of Colyton, with the extended valley ending in the deep blue sea, is particularly good from this point, and well worth a visit to witness.

The short branch railroad to Seaton runs along just below the ruins, and while the navvies were engaged removing some soil in its preparation a massive plain gold ring was discovered, apparently a gift ring: inside is this posy:—

"I esteeme vertue more then gould."

A memorial probably of the palmier-dayed courtesies and amenities of Colcombe.

With the relation of this golden incident, our somewhat extended notice of the old house of Colcombe draws to a close, and curiously enough the termination of our day's wandering seems likely to be fraught with as stormy a finish as that which in days of yore befell the once fair proportions of the ruined edifice before us; for the fierce warmth of the bright sunshine has changed into a sultry oppressive atmosphere, and the god of day, with a sort of angry glance, is retreating behind the opposite hill, enveloped in a kind of incandescent haze, the lurid glow from which penetrates the surrounding cloud gloom, and exhibits the almost sure presage of a coming thunder storm.

So bidding a hasty adieu to our host, we hurry away down the lane toward the quaint little town of Colyton, for the gathering darkness increases rapidly, while a large pile of clouds in the eastern horizon is anon at quick intervals suffused through with intense electric bursts. Quick, friend, to thy heels! for the large drops are whistling through the boughs over head, and every one of them smites through to the skin. But halt!—we cannot out-run the wings of the storm, and forthwith we dart in under the friendly shelter of a hedge-row pollard, whose massive crown is well garnished with a number of thick foliaged boughs, and wait in dry security the termination of the elemental warfare. Two or three vivid flashes of lightning, succeeded by as many rattling peals of thunder, a smart skirmish of hail subsiding into a steady parting shower, and we emerge from our place of refuge in peace.

And now our steps loiter, as the beautiful, sweet, reviving odour rises from the reeking landscape, filling the air with its pleasant freshness. The birds are all silent, but the faithful votive lyrist of eve is in full tune at our feet. Happy insect, think we, as we muse awhile in quiet enjoyment, and string upon the thread of our thoughts these desultory rhymes on the happy destiny of

THE GRASSHOPPER.

Sing on, gay reveller, thy joyous lay,
  For all are voiceless now; no song but thine
Bids welcome to the evening's chastened ray,
  Nor hails the advent of her sway divine;—
But thou her chosen chorister shalt be,
  Deep hidden 'neath the close-wove hedgerow's shade,
To hymn her gentle praise incessantly,
  From every covert dell, and o'ergrown glade.

The day is fled, the broad sunlight is gone,
  His setting smile lurks in yon streak so pale.
And silently, unnoticed, one by one,
  The golden points pierce through the azure veil;
The breeze is whispering through the bending corn,
  Attuning a soft chorus to thy song,
I feel its freshness to my warm cheek borne,
  Flushed now with thought's gay, ceaseless, roving throng.

Who taught thee thus to sing, thou joyous one,
  So merrily at this dark lonely hour?
Or art thou, now the busy day is done,
  Singing thyself to sleep, in some sweet flower?—
Deep mist-hung shadows fill the shady glen,
  The weary leaves are bathed with dewy sheen,
The spider shakes them from his filmy den,
  And hides again beneath his covert green.

That ceaseless song—a jocund heart is thine
  That pours its spirit forth with constant glee,
When the pale glowworm's lamp doth glimmering shine,
  And fays rejoice in festive revelry:
The timid hare steals from her sedgy seat,
  And o'er the level mead is gambolling free,
The beetle hums away on pinion fleet,
  Each wakened by thy song of liberty.

For all is calm, the storm hath passed away,
  No trace is left to mark the blast's rude power,
The rain drops shiver on the trembling spray,
  And chase each other down the drooping flower:—
The bird is slumbering in the tangled bush,
  Leaving to thee the echo of his strain,
And far and wide amid the deepening hush,
  Thy clear "good night" is heard to ring again.

But night is come, and I must haste away,
  Yet still thou singest on untiringly,
Where'er an unknown fate dooms me to stray,
  When skies are dark, I'll strive to think on thee,
And catch the spirit of thy merry song;
  Methinks I hear its cheerful accents still,
Faint on the night wind's sigh borne slow along,
  Joined with the murmuring trickle of the rill.

AXMOUTH

AND ITS

LANDSLIP.

THE most picturesque introduction to the little village of Axmouth is afforded by a view from the opposite side of the river facing its massive church tower, and the scene is not altogether unworthy of an artist's study. The tide is now in; and the river amplified in size for a long distance, has the appearance of an inland lake, and is still and glassy as a mirror. On our left, a pair of graceful dazzlingly white swans are leisurely sailing across—on the right, a large boat full of gaily dressed holiday folks is slowly drifting up the mid stream, the boatmen leisurely resting on their oars. Before us is Axmouth village—a wall or jetty runs out into the water; beside it two or three boats are moored, and behind them at right angles from the river stretches away the broad open village street, skirted with various shaped cottages, the swing sign of the village inn, and a few trees. On the right, apparently on a slight rising ground, and close to the street, rises the really handsome church tower, which is vividly reflected again in the river at its foot, while behind the whole, rampart-crowned, rises the grand hill of Hochsdun forming a massive background. A group of children are at play on the opposite marge — a stray villager or two are moving about the street, and a heavily laden timber carriage drawn by a long string of horses, is creeping steadily along the road leading to the harbour that runs along the other shore of the river.

This to the best of our recollection was the appearance of Axmouth village on a beautiful warm afternoon in early September, as we stepped into our friend's boat and gently ferried ourselves across.

On the opposite shore—and we step out of our little craft close by the group of children who cease their play to look at the strangers. Just six of them are they altogether; one, a young strong girl ten summers old, carrying a great curly pated boy almost as big as herself, whom she was trying to soothe of his fears at our appearance—a dislike he took no pains to conceal, and would not be comforted, as he clasped his sister tightly round the neck, anon turning his head to catch a furtive glance of us, and then burying his face under the curtain of her white tilt bonnet; a second, younger, sat down on the shingle with her arm thrown over the neck of a small wiry-haired terrier, whose erect ears, sparkling eyes and ruffled coat, betokened him as suspiciously inclined as his baby playmate—and three boys, the elder of whom had the object of their amusement dangling by his side—an impromptu ship, fashioned of a long piece of wood with a regiment of stiff feathers stuck in it for masts and sails, which he sailed over the shallow tide secured by a long piece of pack thread for a cable, to insure the safe return of the errant craft back to land again, a piece of nautical venture that evidently awakened the greatest admiration in his companions.

"Well, my little maid," said we, addressing the young nurse, "do you know who keeps the key of the church?"

"'Iss, sir."

"Well, if I give you this," shewing her the larger of our current bronze medallions, "will you go and ask them to let us inside?"

"'Iss, sir,—please sir," said she, holding out one hand for the coin—letting her great child-burthen slide down on his feet with the other—and making a curtsey all in one movement, while at the same instant they all trotted away, the dog busily barking in front, and the ship owner and his companions bringing up the rear.

Axmouth from its appearance, like most settlements on the estuaries of rivers, bespeaks its being a place of great antiquity; a surmise further confirmed by an inspection of its church, which, thanks to the intelligence and nimbleness of our little messenger, we soon enter by the western door in the tower. The massive circular pillars and double arches in the south or Bindon aisle, carry the mind back to the twelfth century, which is further exemplified by the existence of a beautiful Norman arch with its characteristic mouldings in the north porch, now used as a vestry. We proceed up into the chancel, and the fine effigy of the priest in his chasuble, alb and stole, immediately arrests the attention. He was probably one of the early vicars of Axmouth—a monk possibly, from the Priory of Loders, near Bridport, in which house as a cell of the abbey of Montbourg, in Normandy, the patronage of the living was vested; and we find the Priors sometimes inducted themselves, preferring the pleasanter sphere of the country priest's vocation, to the austerities and gloom of conventual life. A curious legend is attached to this figure; and that is, he left a certain piece of ground called "Dog-acre Orchard," (and still known in the parish by that name,) for charitable purposes, as an indemnity for having a favourite dog buried at his feet: the legend further affirming that the animal on which the priest's feet repose is the semblance of that faithful creature. Whether such was ever the case we know not,—but with regard to the dog at this effigy's feet, the dog was generally chosen for the priest to support the feet, as an emblem of fidelity. The tomb beneath this figure was opened and examined some years since, when a skeleton was discovered, the feet were encased in leather boots laced up in front, and which remained very perfect, but no bones of a dog were visible. We pass out into a small side chapel, probably erected as a mortuary one, by some late members of the family possessing Bindon. Here we find a large heavy classic monument to the lady of Sir Thomas Erle, the Parliamentarian captain, and his only son; this was perhaps, his second wife, for it is said Sir Thomas also married a daughter of the celebrated Cromwellian general, Sir William Waller; the inscription is quaint:—

"HEERE LYE THE BODYES OF DAME ANNE ERLE, WIFE OF SIR THOMAS ERLE, AND OF THOMAS ERLE THEIRE ONLY SONNE, AND HEIRE;—TWO RARE PATTERNS, THE ONE FOR HER PIETYE, THE OTHER FOR HIS WISDOME AND ABYLITYES; SHE WAS HEIRE TO FRANCIS DYMMOCK OF ERDINGTON, IN THE COUNTY OF WARWICK, ESQVIRE; THE SONNE DYED JVNE THE 1ST 1650;—THE MOTHER THE 26TH OF JAVRY, 1653."

A very large number of flat stones are found in the aisles inscribed to the antient families of Pyne, with their allusive arms, *three pine cones*—Mallock, Seaward, and one dated 1658, to Elizabeth Wright, *piissimæ matrona*—woman's most coveted and dignified appellation, and before whose loving and sanctified title all other honours sink to insignificance.

After leaving the church, our way takes us up the village street, and we admire the fine clear stream of water that flows through it, similar to one that runs through the opposite village of Beer; and as we arrive at its upper extremity where our path turns off to the right, we halt for a time to examine an old oriel window, and chimney over, on which we see the indication of an inscription, that by the assistance of a small pocket telescope (a most useful help to the travelling antiquary) resolves itself into

"GOD GIVETH ALL."

below which is a wool-pack and merchant's mark, the letters "A. G." and "E. W. G." together with the date "1570." These initials are probably those of Giffard who married one of the daughters and heiresses of Roger Wyke, of Bindon, whose portion of the manor was afterwards acquired by Erle. The old merchant when he built his residence anew, was not disposed to be ashamed of his trade, nor to disown the pious sentiment set above "of Whom come both riches and honour," as well as a righteous reminder to the wayfarer's eye passing along the street. Where do we find examples of such instructive and warning remembrance set up now, on chimney, cornice, or mantel of our modern houses? To be ashamed and hide, alike our vocation and religious sentiment seems to be the unreal effort of the present day, and the object of the greatest solicitude, in our grotesque strivings after fashion and gentility. We believe it was the delightfully gentle and accomplished mind of Ruskin that said in one of his lectures delivered at Edinburgh, in lamenting over the decline of modern art, that it was not to be wondered at, for we had forgotten to dedicate its purest and highest efforts to the glory of Him who is in Himself the Fountain and Creator of all art; and instead of surrounding ourselves with the elevating and beautiful symbolism that would continually remind us of the glory of this great truth in picture and image, we had instead, degraded ourselves by servilely copying and depicting mythological monstrosities and nonentities; and illustrated his view by remarking that if another Vesuvius was to arise that night and overwhelm Edinburgh, as was o'erwhelmed Herculaneum and Pompeii, a stranger digging down a thousand year's hence and exploring drawing-room and boudoir, would say from the teeming Heathen divinities and their associate mythological extravagancies exhibited everywhere for ornamental purposes, and the comparative absence of everything that would give a key to the religious faith of the former inmates—these people were surely all heathens. There is very much more in this home truth than many of us are apt to consider. Our old country mansions were crowded generally with the pictured stories of Holy Writ, set forth in the carved panel of bedstead, cup or table-board, or cunningly worked tapestry; while texts culled from the Sacred Volume displayed themselves on cornice, mantel, porch or chimney; and can we doubt but that these solemn reminders of our Holy Faith that thus met the dweller's eye so continually, must have exercised a wholesomely encouraging or restraining influence on his character and movements. Soon after the Reformation, it was ordered that appropriate texts of Scripture should be "set up" or displayed on the walls of our parish churches, and examples of this excellent practice may yet be seen in those still free from the restorations of modern days. From the church it spread to the home of the worshipper, as we find exemplified in many of the old houses of a cotemporary date left remaining. The chimney before us exhibits it, and there is a notable example on the cornice of an upper room in an old farm house at Hampton, Shute. Listen to the old moralist, who chose the following weighty axioms to meet his fresh-wakened eyes morning by morning, and remind him of life's golden mean during his daily round :—

"KEPE BAKE THIE TONGVE AT MEATE AND MEALE."

"HEE THAT STOPPETH HIS EARE AT THE CRYENGE OF THE PORE, HE SHAL ALSO CRIE AND NOT BE HARDE."*

others similar are found in the neighbourhood, but they are being gradually destroyed, as the old houses are repaired or rebuilt. Even from our modern churches, too, the practice has disappeared, except in very few instances, and the "godly scripture," that manly and plain reminder, that all who run may read, has given place to tortuous mysticisms and obscure

* Proverbs, chapter xxi., verse 13.

symbolism, too often the truthful emblems of the visionary views of faith inculcated therein.

But not only thus in the erection of their homes, did those old fathers of our race display on their dwellings and household stuff such choice allusions to their faith, they inscribed them also on mug and platter—the humble delft and pewter, or more costly silver, and engrafted their sacred imageries and stories on the valuable ornaments that adorned their persons.

One custom too, (now disused, alas!) was surpassingly beautiful. When the old bridegroom of three centuries since, in doublet and trunk hose, *pique devant* beard and ruff; wedded his modest and pretty bride, grandly arrayed in lace cap and stomacher, brocaded kirtle and farthingale, and placed on her trembling finger the massive circlet of gold that tokened their two hearts made that day one—there, within its charmed zone, hidden from the glance of all intruding eyes, was the devout or loving "posy" cunningly engraved, that had ever allusion to the eternity and holiness of the compact and its Founder. How many of these olden "troth-plights" are treasured in families now as heir-looms, with their quaint old godly couplets—here is an example or two, from some preserved in the neighbourhood:—

"In Christ and thee,
My joye shall bee."

—o—

"God did foresee,
We should agree."

—o—

"Fulfilled have we,
God's decree."

"Within my breast,
Thy heart doth rest."

Even up to our grandmother's time almost, this beautiful custom lingered on, but modern "enlightenment" has eschewed it, and correspondingly reduced the grand proportions of these olden golden hoops which were worthy alike of the occasion and its object, to the slender circlets of to-day's use, whose attenuated dimensions preclude the possibility of receiving the posy if wished; and often wear out and require renewal if the good housewife be a busy mistress of many years standing.

A long digression you will say gentle reader; undoubtedly so, we reply, but the subject was inviting, thus looking under the tinsel of our modern notions of things, and gossipping awhile on the circumstance of the old chimney's inscription.

We pursue our way, but not being exactly certain of our proper route, we lift the latch of a cottage door to get information, and immediately are confronted with a venerable dame some seventy summer's off, in a frilled night-cap, with a large pair of circular brass goggles athwart her nose, and in the tremulous treble of age she minutely affords us the requisite particulars, assuring us "that 'tis a good stap out there, tho' she didden think much o' it, once,—but, there! can't expect two vorenoons in one day;" and so thanking our venerable informant we again proceed, following the course of the little brook by the road-side, which seems a sort of paradise for the village ducks that swarm along its rippling precincts.

We halt for a moment to look at Steps House, a long old building, standing picturesquely on the side of the hill, once a residence of importance, but now converted into a row of cottages, and all its olden architectural features obliterated. From this we wind slowly up the Combe passing a venerable farm-house or two on our left by the way, and then turning into a gateway on our right, the path leads us to Bindon, the old manor house of the parish.

Singularly interesting to the visitor is this antient domicile of Bindon, a good representative of the numerous residences erected during the fifteenth and sixteenth centuries by the parochial squires of our County. Though somewhat dilapidated, the venerable hand of Time has dealt tenderly with it, and it still displays a green old age, "frosty but kindly." Of the usual semi-quadrangular form, the left wing exhibits a good elliptic arched doorway, and the adjoining main gateway, an equally fine circular one, shewing the well known amalgam of the expiring Gothic, and its advancing rival the pseudo-classic. Effective gables, numerous strong stone mullioned windows, and compact masonry, conspire to give the appearance of stability and picturesque outline to this old seat of the Wykes and Erles. An invitation from the courteous proprietor to look inside is offered and appreciated. The old building (which appears to have been founded by the Wykes and enlarged by the

Erles) is composed of a large number of rooms, stair-ways, and

"Passages that lead to nothing,"

but one special feature is left, almost unique in its way in this neighbourhood, and that is the chapel or oratory upstairs, and which we take to be the one that Roger Wyke obtained license from Bishop Edmund Lacy on the 16th July, 1425, to "have a chapel within his Manor House, of Bindon, in the Parish of Axmouth," as is stated in that prelate's register.

Having advanced up the main stair-way to the first floor—on the left is a massive oak skreen, close at the base, and with longitudinal trefoil-headed open compartments over. At one end of this, in a pointed arch, a door with a carved traceried head opens to the apartment within. Facing the doorway in the centre of the opposite wall, is a late window with ramified head, now plastered up, but which was originally filled with stained glass. In the eastern jamb of this window, about six feet from the floor, is a large niche richly canopied with tabernacle work; but no patron saint remains, nor can we recover to whom the chapel was dedicated. Below the niche is a small piscina with foliated enrichments. There are no remains of an altar (or *prie dieu*), but its place was probably against the east wall, as the window fronts the south. On the seat of another window near, we observed three carved stone shields *a bouche*, discovered during some repairs, which exhibit the coat-armour of the Wykes—*a chevron ermine, between three birds*—allied apparently with Hody of Nitheway—*argent, a fesse indented within, point in point, vert and sable, between two barrulets sable and vert, a mullet for difference.*

An old and very deep well is found in the adjoining courtyard, from which the water is drawn by the aid of a large wheel; and on an eminence just above the house, is the old manorial barn, a large structure of careful race masonry with long crenelated openings. Tradition speaks of a small massive building that once existed at the rear of the house, and which was employed as a cell or jail for refractory parishioners or other offenders; but we do not learn the lords of the manor were invested with any peculiar legal jurisdiction, and the legend is probably a myth.

Bindon was originally the property of the Bachs, one of whom Nicholas Bach, sold it to Roger Wyke, (a member of the family of Wyke of South Tawton), about the year 1400. In this name it remained until early in the sixteenth century when it became the property of the four daughters and heiresses of Roger Wyke, who married respectively Giffard, Erle, Barry, and Hayes. Walter Erle, the father of Thomas Erle, who married the sister of the Antiquary, lived at Colcombe, Colyton, as we have noticed in our visit to that interesting ruin. He had been attached to the household of King Edward VI., and obtained either by purchase or grant, about the year 1549, the manor, rectory, and advowson of Axmouth; which property at the suppression of monasteries, Henry VIII., gave to his Queen Katharine Parr. The same year he "wedded" at Colyton church, Mary Wyke, one of the heiresses of Roger Wyke of Bindon, where, according to Sir William Pole, he subsequently "dwelt with fayre demesnes there unto belonging," which was enhanced soon after, when his grandson bought his brother-in-law's, Giffard's portion. The succeeding Erles were stirring politicians, and fierce military commanders of the Cromwellian era, whose cause they espoused, and some of their exploits we have noticed at length in our account of Colcombe. They were also active engineers at home, and endeavoured to re-construct their harbour at the mouth of the river. Risdon, writing in 1630, says, "It appeareth divers works have been attempted for the repairing of the old decayed haven; but of late years with better success than formerly, by Thomas Erle, Esq., lord of the land, who, when he had brought the same to some likelihood, was taken away by death, leaving his labours to the unruly ocean; which together with unkind neighbours (by carrying away the stones of that work), made a great ruin of his attempt. But the now lord thereof, his son, hath not only repaired the first ruins, but proceedeth on with purpose to bring to pass that which before him his father intended." Bindon and its demesnes finally passed from the representatives of the Erle family about the middle of the last century.

We now set off for the noted Landslip—that wonderful disruption of the cliffs, which created such consternation at the time of its descent, and still forms one of the most attractive pleasure spots for the visit of the tourist.

Having left the olden manse of Bindon, we pass through a fine level meadow on the plateau of the hill, at present tenanted with a numerous flock of handsome horned sheep; and from thence across an arable field or two of goodly dimensions which slope gently down toward the sea, whose smiling expanse is now in full sight. But where is the Landslip, for no indication of it is visible, although we are certain we must be close on its locality? While we are walking and wondering, all at once the ground falls a little more rapidly, and before we have time to express our surprise, we find ourselves breathless and shuddering on the brink of a precipice some two hundred feet deep—sheer down—and the vast chasm of the Landslip is before us.

Strikingly wonderful is this first view of the great, deep, white, jagged curvilinear crater—broken and serrated on either side into beetling recesses and jutting promontories; while at the bottom, a comparatively broad level portion which fell back from the receding mass, runs along between the cliff-like edges of the rent—slightly undulating, with here and there huge sugar-loaf shaped portions thrust up through the surface to considerable altitude, while at their base between, clusters of scrub and brushwood are growing, and above, the luxurious wild ivy clambering. In front is the bulk of the Landslip proper, some hundred and fifty acres in extent, which leans off detached from the main land toward the sea, traversed and seamed by numerous gaping fissures, and abruptly broken surfaces.

On the left, or Dowlands side, the chasm widens, and the ground slopes gradually toward the sea, but torn and divided into huge boulders and *debris*—the tall white craggy cliffs over are here very fine, and beneath them for a considerable distance onward, there are indications of lesser landslips or disruptions of the cliffs having taken place in former years; but comparatively handfuls in bulk to the one we are now contemplating. On our right, the jaws of the vast crevice narrows abruptly, and tall pinnacles of white rock shoot up at intervals, with great picturesque effect. The whole scene forms a wondrous panorama of wild grandeur—this great battle field of Nature; where, leagued with his sparkling Nereids, the powerfully insidious hand of Neptune has undermined and sought to possess himself of the spoils of Titan. The visitor accustomed to the more smiling and peaceful aspects of Nature will do well to witness this scene of energy and desolation,—it will not be easily forgotten.

Having gazed with a kind of unsatisfied pleasure and wonder, on the tumultuously incidented scene below, we seat ourselves down awhile on a most inviting green hillock just at our rear, while our eyes seek repose for a season on the calm and shining ocean which is laid out in vast amplitude in our front, bounded on the one side by the receding range of South Devon cliff-land, and on the other by the long wedge-shaped promontory of

PORTLAND.

Descried far out at sea, near where the main
Of ocean mingles with the fleecy cloud,
Thy glistening cliffs, gaunt Portland firm remain
A massive barrier to the waters proud.

While stretching from thy base in snake-like rift
The Chesil heaves her bosom to the sea,
On which the wavelets play with curling drift,
'Till laid in foam low at the foot of thee.

The laden bark sweeps by thy coast with care
Shunning that spot where circling eddies meet,
Attentive marks thy beacon from afar,
And rounds thy point with satisfaction sweet.

We descend into the interior of the chasm—this raid into the bowels of the earth as it were. The great immensity of this stupendous piece of Nature's engineering bursts at once upon the sight, and the puny works of man, seem comparatively like dust upon the balance. Endless picturesque combinations charm the eye, especially toward the western termination of the chasm, and the towering altitude of its cliff-like sides, give the scene a grand and almost awful import; while the roughened surfaces, although somewhat worn and denuded of their original ruggedness, are still very wild and imposing. We thread our way carefully along over the huge ledges, and by the boulder-shaped massss, the *disjecta membra* of the wonderful convulsion—catching sight occasionally of a small pair of long ears poised erect for a moment, and then a small grey body, followed by a second or third companion that seem to rise out of the earth, then speeding swiftly away, to their place of refuge, "the stony rocks for the conies."

Wending on our path thus, we find ourselves at last down by the rippling shore, where we are again glad to rest awhile, for the walk is sufficiently fatiguing. There is not much other than ordinary to be observed here now, beyond the additional protuberance of the large bulk of the shattered cliff thrust forward into the sea—when the landslip first occurred, a large mound or reef of beach was thrown up outside, near a mile long; inside which, at each extremity, was formed a considerable sized lake of salt water, but this gradually subsided into the ocean again. Various theories were propounded at the time of its descent—some alarmists asserting that nothing less than an earthquake could have caused such a severance—but eminent geologists who visited the spot came to the conclusion which common sense would at once endorse, that beneath the visible strata of chalk, flint, and sandstone, there exists a bed of loose sand, well known as "fox-mould," that the land springs washing down and out through this on the one hand, (as the fox-mould rests on the impermeable lias, which prevents the descent of the water further,) and the fret of the tide beneath on the other, culminated in the course of time, in the enormous slip of the superincumbent mass forward into the sea.

An almost unexampled field of research and investigation was displayed to the scrutiny of the geologist—specimens of the ammonite, belemnite, and other fossils occurring in the lias formation were exhumed in great profusion, and eagerly appropriated by the crowds of savans, and other ordinary visitors who thronged to the scene of desolation in immense numbers from all parts of the kingdom on hearing of this extraordinary occurrence.

The exact period of the descent, was on the night succeeding Christmas Day, 1839, and it continued gradually sinking or subsiding during the whole of the next day. There was no noise of any kind except from portions of the detached soil falling down. An eye witness who was present on the morning following the descent, and while the mass was still settling, describes the scene as being of a very awful description; to see the vast and apparently bottomless cracks extending, and the mass of land moving, while as if to shroud this vast convulsion in still further mystery, there was a dense fog setting in from the sea, enveloping everything.

PSALM, LXXVII. VERSE, 19.

"Thy way is in the sea, and Thy path in the great waters, and Thy footsteps are not known."

Who may compare with Thee—Thou wondrous Power,
Benign to bind the mourner's breaking heart,
Or strong to rend at the lone midnight hour,
Alike unseen,—these sundered cliffs apart,—
Who know the errand of Thy viewless hand,
Or stay the bidding of Thy great command?

The tiny works of man, like ant-heaps raised
On this green meadow, or yon plough-shares trace,
Speak of his finite purpose,—here, amazed
We bow where strength Infinite hath a place,
Thy "unknown footstep," that doth grandly bide,
Graven for ever on the earth and tide.

Thou who dost poise the planet in the air,—
Rend cliff and scar,—bid the fierce whirlwind rush,—
The vast waves whelm,—the gleaming lightnings tear,—
Or gentlest reign, as now when eve's soft hush
With roseate tints soothes the bright bier of day
Ere purple languors cradle its decay.

As we regained the crest of the chasm on our return, we were fortunate to witness a most splendid and imposing sunset. The gloaming of evening had set in, and covered the wide expanse of sea and land before us with that indefinable grey neutral tint, so soft and pleasing, and which clothes sea, hill, valley, cliff, cape, and cloud-land alike with slightly differing depths of the same colour. In the west, the long promontory of the Start receded back till its furthermost point was lost in the distance; on the undulating hill line, a long bank of dim cloud seemed to rest, and in its centre, tempered of his golden day-blaze, the large crimson glowing disc of the sun was slowly sinking, traversed across with two or three narrow cloud streaks, semblancing in some wise a huge embodiment of the planet Mars, banded with the belts of Jupiter. Immediately over, uprose a soft halo of light, which extended itself high into the calm sky, embodying and blending indescribably every shade of crimson, yellow, pale green, and violet in imperceptible gradation of tint. With majestic splendour the burning rim insensibly lessened, and finally disappeared, drawing the attendant corona of glory after it. Our steps were rapidly conveying us homeward, while we were watching the sublime heavenly pageant, and as we turned for an instant to look our last at the calm serene expanse now fast settling into shadow ere we descended into the lane—the tall signal post of the coast guard watchmen on Haven Cliff was faintly reflecting the last trace of day, and, as if to bid us a last adieu, a gull with broad white wings broke through the gloom, and after balancing himself an instant over the beetling head-land, dropped measuredly down to his cliffy home. Chastened thoughts crowd on our heart as we watch the retreating glance of those bright pinions, and remember one that delighted to sing of them, and who, after drinking his full meed of sorrow in this life—too oft the poet's portion—is now laid at rest in the little churchyard in the valley below.

Our Wanderings, gentle reader, have for the present, come to their conclusion. We started on our pleasant peregrinations on a bright sunny morning from the opposite bank of the sweet river before us then dressed by the morning sun with ten thousand glittering flashes; and after making a delightful circuit through the adjacent neighbourhood—lingering among its endless natural beauties by woodland, mead, hill-top, and river—invoking from the Past a new acquaintanceship with the mighty names whose fame has floated onward upon the stream of Time to the Present—and halting and meditating among the crumbling vestiges of former human activities, as we conjured afresh their olden histories,—so have we wandered, until now we stand at our journey's end, on the opposite brink of the gentle river,—when the evening shadows have wrapped its silent flow in chastened gloom; but bright star-sparkles are striking deep into its glassy bosom beneath us, and the last traces of daylight reflected from over the distant hill, are quivering faintly on its farther marge—its lingering adieu, and silent promise of a coming morrow.

Strange but apt symbol of that longer and more eventful wandering of life, which thou, gentle reader in company with ourselves are adjourneying,—may its round be as pleasant, and its finish as calm and hopeful.

We reach the harbour, are quietly ferried across, and again the healing spirit of the muse comes to our rescue, as the flight of those ghost-like wings recurs to the eye of memory, evoking, from her lyre a sympathetic echo; here is its burthen of inspiration:—

THE GULL.

O solitary gull, that sweepest round
Yon beetling crag, surf-gnawed by endless seas,
Now lessening slow toward the horizon's bound,
Like snow-flake balanced on the winter breeze,
I watch with musings deep your measured flight,
And follow on imaginations pinions light.

Thy bright full eye looks o'er the pulsing waste,
Where dark lines eddying chase the sunbeam's flash,
Or scans clear depths, where quivering glance and haste
Pearl-coated forms quick as the lightning's dash;
Or views eve's Iris splendours slow decay
Where the lone shadowy sail moves on her way.

So I, like thee, far o'er the sea of thought,
Fly circling oft around life's rugged rock,
Gaze down its charmed depths with bright forms fraught,
Or stretch away where Fancy's marvels mock
This dull earth haunting round, that ever more,
Bears leaden impress of its wearying shore.

THE END.

www.ingramcontent.com/pod-product-compliance
Lightning Source LLC
Chambersburg PA
CBHW020620030726
47497CB00007B/2330

* 9 7 8 3 3 3 7 1 8 9 8 8 4 *